The Valorous Years

A. J. CRONIN

A. J. Cornell Publications
New York

5⁄24

For information address:
A. J. Cornell Publications
18-74 Corporal Kennedy St.
Bayside, NY 11360

Cover illustration by Gordon King

Cover design by Jonathan Gullery

Library of Congress Control Number: 2009907315

ISBN: 978-0-9727439-7-6

Printed in the Unites States of America

CHAPTER 1

When it was too late to turn back, he saw her on the upper slope of the meadow. Hitching up his heavy creel with his good arm, he walked steadily downstream. But her dogs spied his.

"Duncan! Hello, Duncan!"

Her call halted him, and he turned. She was pretty in her short tweed skirt and brogues, her soft hair shining in the slanting sunshine.

"Well!" The word was a reproach, a reprimand for his attempted flight.

"Margaret!" He kept his excuse even. "I scarcely heard you."

She smiled provokingly, both hands on her shooting stick, and studied his queer, shabby figure, the square forehead, the deep-set, uncommunicative eyes. "Dr. Overton is fishing. I came to meet him. Have you seen him?"

He shook his head, and she laughed.

"You're not very talkative, Duncan, for a boy I went to school with. I believe the thought of your grand new appointment has gone to your head!"

With effort he saved himself from wincing and nodded in agreement. "A fine chance, isn't it?"

"You haven't got it yet," she teased. "Not till the meeting this evening." She stopped, relenting. "Here's something that'll bring you luck. I found it on the hill as I walked over." She held out a sprig of early white heather.

"Thank you, Margaret." His voice shook as he took it with his left hand, fumbled it into the pocket of his coat.

At that moment someone shouted behind them. Overton, clambering up the riverbank, waved his rod in greeting. He drew near, his neat, handsome features dewed with perspiration from the short ascent.

"Why, Margaret, you wretch! I've been hunting you these

last two hours. What d'you mean, leaving your distinguished guest?" As an afterthought he acknowledged Duncan. "'Evening, Stirling. Any luck?"

"Nothing to speak of." Duncan was instantly antagonized. This pretentious upstart, whom he had surpassed in every class at school, still treated him with condescension.

"Nothing at all, I suppose." Dr. Overton peered into the other's creel, then involuntarily exclaimed: "Good Lord! What's this? Five—six pounders. And I haven't got one."

"Would you care to have a trout?"

"Why, yes!" Delighted, Overton swung around. "I'd love some."

"Take them all," Duncan said pleasantly.

"My dear fellow, that's sporting of you. You're sure?"

"Quite sure. I can get trout whenever I want them."

All Duncan's self-restraint could not keep contempt from his tone; but Overton, busy transferring the speckled fish to his own creel, was oblivious.

He chuckled, turning to Margaret. "I'll enjoy watching your father's face when he sees what I've brought in."

"But, Euen," Margaret protested mildly, "you didn't catch them."

"All's fair in love and fishing." He looked at her meaningly.

Duncan shifted his sodden feet. "Time for me to be getting along."

He whistled to Rust, who lay crouched in the low bracken. As the dog moved, a sudden thought struck Overton.

"Is that the dog?" he asked.

"That's the one."

"You've made quite a job."

Margaret shuddered in recollection. "After the truck went over him, he must have been in pieces!"

"He was," Duncan answered quietly. "But somehow they came together again."

"You should specialize in jigsaw puzzles." Overton dismissed the subject with a grin. "Well, I probably won't see you again. I'm due back at the University next Thursday for the Lockhart Examination."

"The Bursaries?" Duncan queried.

"The same." Overton looked important. "One of the woes of a lecturer of St. Andrews! Superintending seven hundred would-be doctors every spring."

"It's a wonder you survive!" The words were so quiet that the bitterness behind them passed unobserved. And the next instant Duncan had raised his hat to Margaret and gone on his way.

They stood looking after him.

"Queer young devil, isn't he, Marge?"

"You'd be queer, too, if you had a handicap like that, wouldn't you—" she smiled at him—"my dear?"

Throughout the long walk to town, Duncan miserably pictured Margaret and Overton strolling together to Stinchar Lodge, the home of Margaret's father, Colonel Scott. He saw the great hall with a log fire blazing. A manservant in dull-green livery would bring tea. When Overton's father dropped in—Honest Joe Overton, contractor and iron founder, the richest man in Levenford—Margaret would pour, and young Overton would move about the room handing cups, bragging about his impressive catch.

Euen Overton had the knack, always, of appearing to advantage. An only son, spoiled by Honest Joe, his lavish allowance gave him a cocksure arrogance. If his manner were showy rather than well-bred, he concealed it cleverly with a disarming smile.

Duncan remembered how often, swiftly and shamefully, he had glanced through the windows of that same hall, when, years ago, he had delivered groceries to the great house. True, he and Margaret had been at school together; but in these northern towns, the local academy served both the Laird's pretty daughter and the charwoman's deformed son.

He reached the ugly town of Levenford, sprawling between the dirty estuary and the steelworks, which fringed the railway station, and turned at length into a mean and narrow street, filled with the sights and smells of poverty. How well he knew them!

He paused at a dark side entrance, lifted the latch of a familiar door, and entered his home. Here, in contrast to the world outside, were spotlessness and quiet.

His father was in his corner seat, most unusually sober. For the past ten days, in honor of the great event now due, Long Tom Stirling had maintained an anguished abstinence.

"You're back," he commented cautiously, nursing the bowl of his clay pipe in the palms of his hands. "Your mother's in the parlor setting supper."

A look passed between the two men—a flash, momentary and elusive in the little gaslit room, yet charged with understanding. Long Tom Stirling was the town loafer. The town drunkard. Thirty years before, he had been a spry enough young man, Clerk to the Borough Council, school janitor, caretaker in Levenford Hall. Now his long, lean, dilapidated figure ranged between the steps outside the Red Lion Inn and the bar within. For a quarter of a century he had done no work. Yet his one son loved him.

"It's the fatted calf for ye tonight," whispered Long Tom. "I haven't seen your mother so worked up over anything in years."

Duncan stared darkly into the blink of fire in the grate, seeing the hopelessness of his future, the inevitable closing of every avenue of escape. Suddenly, at a faint sound, he swung around, to find his mother gazing at him.

"Your blue suit is pressed and on your bed upstairs, Duncan. And I've laid out a clean stiff shirt and collar. You must look your best tonight."

"My best!" He could not keep the resentment from his voice.

Her lips drew in, but she made no reply. It was strange how in her silence she dominated the room. A small woman was Martha Stirling, dressed in worn-out black, with a pale and deep-lined face. Her hands, clasped beneath her bodice, were red and seamed and knotted. They were eloquent of twenty-five years of toil, an endless sequence of soapy water, of scrubbed floors, of a thousand washings, manglings, launderings, by which, fiercely, indomitably, piously, she had supported her shiftless husband and reared her beloved son.

"I'll have a nice supper for you when you come back." The faint relaxation of her sternness showed the tenderness, the pride she felt in him. "I expect ye'll deserve it."

Unexpectedly the bonds of his restraint snapped. He spoke rapidly, with the reckless urgency of despair. "It's hard to say this, Mother, but I must tell you—I don't want to apply for this post."

"And why not?" The question cut like a whip.

"Because I hate the work!"

"You hate the work?" She repeated it incredulously.

"It's petty and useless; it leads nowhere. If I take it, I'm stuck for life!"

"Stop!" She drew her breath in sharply. "It's a sorry day when I hear the position of Clerk to the Council so miscalled! What work would ye have, indeed?"

He answered passionately, "You know what I've always wanted to do."

A light of understanding broke upon her face, and she was calm. She spoke pityingly, as if soothing him from a wild and childish dream. "My poor Duncan! I thought you'd put that nonsense from your head for good. You must remember your position in life. We're poor working people. And even if we had money for what ye're set on—" Her voice was touched with a deeper pity. "I know what's best for ye, my son. All these years I've worked and prayed that ye might one day hold the respectable position your father was weak enough to disgrace. And now it's like to come to pass." She dismissed the matter with a movement of her head. "Go up and change now, son. It would ill befit you to be late."

He stifled a torrent of entreaty. After all, was she not right? What could he do, limited as he was in money and physique? He turned and went upstairs.

There, in the attic that was his own, his eyes strayed to the textbooks he had studied so painstakingly, so fruitlessly, into the midnight hours. Tears came hot and stinging to his eyes.

CHAPTER 2

Seated on the hard bench in the anteroom of the Council Chamber, Duncan heard the prosy voices, and his bitterness hardened within him.

What did it matter—his desperate, unquenchable ambition? What did it matter—his own capacity, recognized deep within him, the hidden faculty that motivated every thought, every aspiration of his life? He knew that he possessed a rare gift. Rust, the shattered dog, had come back to life under his hand. Once, at play, a schoolmate had wrenched a shoulder from its socket. Duncan remembered vividly how he had reduced the dislocation and relieved the screaming child with a few movements of his one good hand.

The door opened. Todd, the porter, made a sign.

Through the haze of tobacco smoke Duncan saw the Councillors at the long oak table, felt the battery of their eyes greeted full upon him. Presiding at the board was Margaret's father, Colonel Scott, and his was a kindly gaze. There sat Troup, the undertaker, Leggat, the lawyer, Simpson, the parson—small-town nobodies. But the last member of the Committee was no nonentity; Honest Joe Overton, self-made magnate, pillar of the church, whose industrial adventures extended over half the countryside. And as Duncan sustained the veiled, appraising eye of the contractor, he knew that there he had an enemy.

Colonel Scott was first to speak. He smiled at Duncan to put him at ease. "Glad to see you here, Stirling. . . . Well, gentlemen, here, I trust, is our new Clerk to the Council."

"Not so fast, Mr. Chairman," It was Honest Joe. "This appointment touches us closely. We ought to sum up the qualifications of the candidate."

Leggat, cocking his pointed beard, remarked slyly, "Haven't they been summed up for us already by a member of the candidate's family?"

The mild titter at the lawyer's innuendo sent the blood to Duncan's head. He knew that his mother, in her anxiety, had gone to every Committeeman to beg the post for him.

"Gentlemen, please!" The Colonel rapped on the table. "We all know Duncan Stirling. It's merely a question of affirming our choice."

"All very fine, John!" Overton leaned back. "But in my business, when I buy an article, I want a sound article."

"Come, come, Joe!" The Colonel frowned. "The work's purely clerical."

"How did you get the deformity, Stirling?" Troup, the wizened little undertaker, studying the candidate with professional eyes, morbidly threw out the question.

Checking the indignant answer quivering on his lips, Duncan replied, "I had poliomyelitis when I was twelve."

"Polio—what?"

"Infantile paralysis, you fool," growled the Colonel. He turned to Duncan. "You're aware of the conditions of the appointment. A five-year agreement, capable of extension—" he smiled—"which means it's practically for life. And a salary beginning at thirty shillings a week."

CHAPTER 3

"Wait a minute, if you please!" Overton thumped the table with his fist. They were afraid of him, and he reveled in the knowledge of his power. "I still question whether the candidate is fit for the job. Don't forget, we often have serious private matters to discuss." He paused meaningly. "When I go ahead with my big Linton power scheme, in which ye'll all be interested, we'll need a reliable clerk."

"True!" agreed Simpson, the parson, with a sanctimonious uplift of his eyes.

"Exactly!" Overton nodded. "And there's another point I want to raise. The candidate's father, who once held this position—what guaranty have we that his son'll not turn out the same way?"

There was a dead silence. Duncan felt a burning wave sweep over him. He realized clearly the reason for the other's venom. Ever since, as a boy at the academy, he had dared to outrank Euen Overton, the rich man's precious son, the local potentate had held a grudge against him.

His nerves, taut from weeks of brooding, tortured by this cruel cross-examination, seemed to snap. He faced Honest Joe with white, defiant carelessness.

"What about your own morals?" Duncan's voice strengthened, hardened. "You set yourselves up as guardians of the community. All the time you're looking for nothing but personal profit."

"That's a slander on the Committee," shouted Overton.

"Is it?" Duncan shouted back. "What about your profit on the land you bought for a song and resold to the town as the gasworks site?"

"It's a damned lie!" protested Overton, reddening with anger.

"The twenty thousand you made out of the town library, built with your rotten bricks and mortar, and the contract you drew yourself—is that another lie?"

"Really, really," piped Troup in a panic, "do we have to put up with this?"

Duncan spun around fiercely. "You're in the racket, too, and the whole town knows it. You even make two hundred percent profit on the matchboard coffins you sell the work-house."

There was a stricken silence in the Council Chamber. Then the hubbub arose.

Vainly Colonel Scott tried to curb the opposition, to rally the forces in favor of Duncan. "Gentlemen, gentlemen! We mustn't be too touchy. It's the privilege of youth to speak its mind."

He was overborne. Overton had regained his tongue. Tugging at his collar, he shouted: "You'll never get this position! Not if you live to be a hundred!"

"I don't want it!" Duncan shouted back. For the present, at least, he did not care. "I'd rather starve, and keep my self-respect!"

"You'll starve, all right," bawled Overton, brandishing his fist. "You're finished in Levenford! You'll remember this evening when you're crawling in the gutter, whining for charity."

"You'll remember it, too," cried Duncan, "when my name's known the world over!"

It left them speechless. They gaped at him.

CHAPTER 4

Parked at the entrance, when Duncan emerged, was Colonel Scott's runabout with Margaret at the wheel, waiting to drive her father home. She signaled frantically. There were tears of laughter in her eyes.

"Duncan!" She exclaimed. "Neil Todd just told me. He listened at the keyhole. I'm hysterical, really, when I think of it—" She shook with laughter.

Throbbing from his painful experience, the set of his jaw still hard, he watched her with a queer hurt that she should transmute his tragedy to farce. He said somberly, "It isn't such a joke for me."

"No, no." She paused. "Still, perhaps it was rather stupid, refusing the position. What on earth are you going to do?"

"I don't know." He clenched his hand. "Except maybe—start to fight!"

She gazed at him in wry interrogation. Speculation grew in her bright blue eyes.

He looked at her intently. How lovely she was, how naturally perfect, the princess in the far-off tower. His determination grew; a sudden desire to tell her his hopes flooded his heart. He found himself saying urgently: "Margaret, don't laugh at me. I've always—all my life—wanted to be a doctor. I know I have it in me to heal people—to be a success in medicine." Before she could raise the inevitable objection, he hurried on. "I know I'm handicapped, but that wouldn't prevent me. I could be the finest doctor of them all!"

"Shouldn't you have thought of this before?"

"I have. I've thought of it till I'm half-crazy."

There was a silence. Aware of what this must mean to Duncan, the girl was embarrassed, beyond her depth. She temporized vaguely. "If only you could have gone to the University of St. Andrews. Dr. Overton might have helped. We could have written to my uncle, who's Dean of the Faculty there."

The interest in her words lifted him. He said: "It's good of you to want to help me. But I have a plan. It's been in my mind for months."

"What is it?"

"It's madness," he answered slowly. "Don't ask me any more. There's one chance in a million it'll work."

Again the silence. Then she smiled prettily, touched his shoulder lightly, reassuringly. "Something will turn up, I'm sure. Goodness! The light's out in the Committee Room. That means they've broken up. Heavens, Duncan! You mustn't let them find you here!"

It was not the way he wanted to leave her, yet he knew he must not compromise her by remaining. He wished he could express in one swift phrase everything he felt toward her. But words were seldom ready to his tongue. He clasped her hand, stammered a conventional farewell.

CHAPTER 5

By the time he reached home, he was filled with feverish excitement. As he entered the kitchen, his father stopped rocking in the corner chair.

"Your mother went out to meet you twenty minutes ago. Couldn't wait to hear the good news."

"Good news!"

In a few words, he told what had happened. A strange, impressive silence fell, broken only by the slow ticktock of the old clock on the wall. Then Long Tom rose stiffly from his chair, slowly extended his hand, and gave his son a long, firm clasp. Nothing was said, yet the pause that followed was eloquent.

Finally Duncan said vehemently, "It's important, isn't it, Dad, to do what you want to do?"

"It is, my boy."

"Dad!" Duncan said. "On Thursday of next week they're holding the Lockhart Bursary Examination at the University of St. Andrews. It's an open competition—anybody can enter, from a duke's son to somebody like me. Three scholarships are awarded. And any one of them means freedom— freedom to study medicine!" He stopped for breath and then rushed on. "I don't say I have a chance, but I'm going to try if it kills me!"

Long Tom contemplated his son from beneath his sandy brows, a secret gaze in which pride was strangely mingled. Then he filled two glasses with whisky and held his aloft.

"I'll give ye my toast, my son! To Duncan Stirling, M.D.—in ten years' time, the finest doctor in the kingdom. And the devil take those who deny it!" He downed the liquor in a single draught, then shattered the glass on the hearth.

At that instant the front door banged open, a blast of wind blew into the warm living room, and following it came the mistress of the house. Martha Stirling stood tense and pale in the doorway. Her blazing eyes saw the whisky on the table. Her lips were tightly compressed.

"It seems I have disturbed you," she said.

Long Tom, disconcerted, muttered an apology.

"I might have expected this of you," she said bitterly, "but to drag your son down with you!"

"Mother!" Duncan stepped forward protestingly. "Be careful what you say!"

"And were you careful what you said?"

So she knew. They faced each other for a dreadful moment. Then the torrent of her speech broke free.

"Never would I have believed it of a son of mine! After all I've hoped and prayed for! There's only one thing to be done. You must go to Mr. Overton and take back what you've said——"

"I won't take it back," he interrupted. "Not a word of it. I'm sorry to hurt you, Mother, but my mind's made up."

Sensing the thought behind his steady gaze, she cried, "Is it that same madness about doctoring?"

He nodded.

Anger and disappointment almost mastered her. She could not bear it, this obsession he had, she who had his welfare, his future at heart. "For the last time, will you apologize to the Committee?"

"No, Mother."

"Then I'm done with you!" She rushed on. "You'll leave this house tonight. And once you've left it——don't come back!"

Long Tom, standing dumbly between his wife and son, made a quick protest. But she swept it relentlessly aside.

"I mean it! If you go now, you go for good!"

For a long, still moment Duncan's eyes remained upon her. Then he said quietly, "It's as you say, Mother."

Paralyzed with bitterness and disappointment, the woman remained immobile.

Upstairs, in his room, the boy made a bundle of his books and clothing. In the little hall, when he came down, he found his father and the dog awaiting him.

Clearing his throat huskily, Long Tom fumbled in his waistcoat pocket. "I want you to take something, Duncan lad. It isn't much. I haven't any money, but at least I have got this."

It was his watch and chain, which had been his father's before him, the watch of gold, the chain of heavy silver, an heirloom treasured through the years and never pawned despite the urge of poverty.

"No," protested Duncan. "I can't."

Long Tom forced the token on his son, stifling gratitude with a pressure of his hand. "Good-bye, son, and good luck."

"Good-bye, Dad." Duncan shouldered his pack. "Good-bye, Mother," he called out to the kitchen.

There was no reply.

CHAPTER 6

It was ninety miles by road from Levenford to St. Andrews, and Duncan walked twenty of them that night. Toward four in the morning he flung himself down in the lee of a haystack. With eyes fixed on the pale sliver of moon over which ragged clouds raced wildly, he could not sleep. In his pockets he had only a few coins. He had thrown away his past; the avenues of return to his home were closed. The more he brooded, the more he saw himself a presumptuous fool, casting loaded dice with Destiny. But his courage remained.

Next day he covered thirty miles, keeping free of the towns, using country paths and hillside tracks. At noon he bought some biscuits in a village shop, made a frugal meal with deep draughts of spring water from a nearby well. The country was superb, a rugged skyline of mountain peaks clothed in pine and gorse, green pastures on the lower slopes, through which peat-stained streams went tumbling in gay cataracts toward the plain below. Here and there were dotted whitewashed farmhouses, little cultivated crofts. Near the road a flock of sheep moved peacefully. It was Perthshire at its best, the lovely valley of Strath Linton.

But in the afternoon, midway through the glen, Duncan Stirling felt the touch of rain. Soon he was walking in a deluge; a wind arose, chilling him to the bone.

When dusk was falling, he reached the village of Linton. The single street was deserted; post office and stores were already closed; all doors were shut against the weather. Deciding he could go no farther, Duncan twice trudged up and down the forlorn thoroughfare, seeking shelter for the night. At length he stopped before the local doctor's house, a comfortable, gray-stone dwelling, and contemplated the nameplate on the gate: DR. ANGUS MURDOCH, PHYSICIAN AND SURGEON.

There was an outbuilding adjacent to the house, with a deep archway that seemed partly dry. He strode into the archway, settled his pack, and propped himself up, shivering, in a corner.

Hardly had he done so when the door opened, and a girl, with a plaid thrown over her head, darted for the shelter of the house. Almost colliding with him, she stopped, observed him with unstartled surprise.

"I'm sorry! I took the liberty of sheltering a moment in your—"

"Chicken house." She supplied the word gravely, her steady eyes intent upon his face. "I've just been feeding them." She added with the same simplicity: "You're very wet. Come in and shelter in the kitchen."

"No, no." His pride made him refuse; but she insisted.

CHAPTER 7

He followed her across the yard, where, even in the rain, he could see a carefully tended garden. She opened the back door of the house, showed him into the kitchen. A small Highland maid rose at their entrance.

"Sit down by the fire," the girl said. "When your clothes are dry, we'll give you a meal. Then, if you wish, you can go on your way."

Duncan obeyed, watching her. She was about eighteen, he judged; neat and trim, with a lovely, compact figure. Her complexion had the creamy warmth of perfect health. She was dark, her hair arranged with simplicity. Her eyes were her most striking feature: deep, dark brown, holding a rare tranquility.

In Duncan's present mood, her calmness irritated him. "Do you often entertain tramps who pass this way?" he asked.

"We do. In fact, I thought you were one till you came in. But tramps are never cheeky—until they're fed."

"I wasn't aware I'd indicated I was hungry."

"You are hungry. Don't deny it."

He fought down a queer confusion. It was comfortable in the kitchen, and the smell of dinner cooking struck him forcefully.

"What brings you to these parts?" she inquired. Her kind young eyes were friendly. "I wish you'd tell me who you are and where you're going."

He felt a quick affection, as though she were a younger sister. And he said, "I'm going to St. Andrews College!"

"To study?" Her eyes brightened. "What?"

Cornered, he answered, "Medicine."

She clapped her hands. "Isn't that grand! Father'll be interested when you tell him. He'll be back any minute now from his round."

"He's the doctor here?" Duncan asked.

She made a gesture of assent. "The only one for miles around."

Outside, there was the crunch of wheels on gravel, the slam of an automobile door. A minute later Dr. Murdoch came in.

He was a short, bristling, red-faced bulldog of a man, perhaps sixty years of age, beaten by weather, battered by work and time—his mustache gray, and gray his piercing eyes. An old shooting cap sat upon his ears; his figure was swathed in an enormous checked cape, which almost reached his heavy boots.

"Jean! Jean! Is dinner ready?" he demanded. "I'm that sharp set I could eat an ox!" Suddenly he became aware of Duncan, stopped short in his tracks, and eyed the stranger up and down. As he stripped his cape from his shoulders, he continued the scrutiny.

"What's this we have! Another dead beat, by the look of him. Jean! Ye'll be the end of me with your ever-open door. Just a youngster, too! God bless my soul!" Then, "Well, sir, what have you to say for yourself?"

"Nothing!" Duncan had risen, his expression gradually hardening during the brief harangue.

"Am I to be nothinged on my own hearthstone by a youngster that the wind blew into my kitchen?" the old doctor barked.

"I can blow out as fast as I blew in." Duncan took a step toward the door.

"Stop!" roared Murdoch. "You headstrong young fool! D'you think I'd let man or beast gang out in such a night? I was just joking. But Lord in Heaven, ye have a temper." The gray eyes twinkled. "And by my soul, I like ye for it."

CHAPTER 8

Slowly Duncan came away from the door. Suddenly he felt faint and giddy. He swayed, shook with a fit of shivering until his teeth chattered.

Murdoch went forward swiftly, guided him to a chair. Now his tone was gentle. "This'll never do. We'll have you with pneumonia unless you change. Jean! Run up and get some things of mine."

The comfort of the warm, dry clothes surpassed all understanding. When Duncan had them on, had washed his face and hands in hot water, he felt a new man, except that he was starving. Shrewdly the old doctor scanned his guest.

"Supper's ready, I'll wager. To make up for all your brag and blow, bless my soul if I don't make ye eat it with us in the parlor."

At first, as Duncan sat down at table with Dr. Murdoch and his daughter, he was stiff and awkward. But when the meal was served, he forgot all else, fell to, and ate as he never had before. Scots broth came first, followed by a gigot, tender and juicy, of the glen's best mountain mutton. Baked potatoes and turnips from the doctor's own garden flanked the joint. Afterward there was gooseberry tart, served with clotted cream that clung to the spoon from goodness.

An odd pity misted the old doctor's gaze as he covertly observed his guest. He glanced meaningly, inquiringly, at his daughter. Said he: "Some more cream, Mr.— Bless me if I caught the name."

Stirling is the name," muttered Duncan. "Duncan Stirling."

"Duncan Stirling," repeated the other. Well, it's a good Scots name, thank God, though ye are a contrary young de'il. Come on. There's nothing like a good dinner to put new heart in a man."

22

At last Duncan sighed contentedly. Then, with a quick, shamefaced glance at his host, he said, "I'm afraid I was sharp." Murdoch made a clucking noise with his tongue. "Ye but followed my one and only prescription: Feed a cold and starve a colic!"

Jean was moved to laughter, at the way the old man said it with his head slyly on one side. "I'm sorry, Father," she said contritely. "But speaking of prescriptions, Mr. Stirling's going to St. Andrews to be a medical student."

"What!" Dr. Murdoch scrutinized his visitor once again. "So?" he said.

Duncan met his eyes unwaveringly. "Crooked arm and all, I'm going to try."

"Your classes are all arranged for?"

"To the last detail."

"And—er—paid for?"

Duncan smiled. "I'm surprised at you, Dr. Murdoch. Would you expect me to get tuition free at a Scots university?"

"No, no." Murdoch's smile was equally bland. "That's just the point—I wouldn't." And to himself he thought, "God, there's something about this proud, half-starved young scarecrow that minds me of long ago, and of a lad named Angus Murdoch." Aloud he said: "Occasionally we're in St. Andrews, Jean and I. I buy my drugs there and a few books." He waved his hand toward the room's many shelves. "When we come in, we'll look you up. Where will you be stopping?"

Duncan hesitated. "I—I haven't made up my mind yet. I must ask the Dean to recommend lodgings."

"So ye know Dr. Inglis?" Murdoch continued. "That's fine. I know him well myself. Wherever ye land, we're sure to find ye."

Duncan saw that the shrewd old doctor was finding him out. But unexpectedly Murdoch switched the subject.

"Speaking of books," said he, "if ye're anything of a scholar, let me show you something a poor man's not ashamed of."

As Jean left the room to visit her kitchen, he rose, and, moving around his shelves, kept Duncan interested for an hour with his beloved folios.

In the end he laid his hand on Duncan's shoulder. "You're spending the night here. Jean has your room all ready. And Hamish'll drive ye to St. Andrews tomorrow." He stopped Duncan's stumbling thanks with a quick pressure of his arm. Don't say it. Ye're more than welcome! I'll bid ye good-night, myself. It's late. And, besides, I'll wager a sixpence to a guinea that they'll have me out tonight. There's a new bairn expected at Davisons' at the head of the Strath. I've brought five into the world there. I wouldn't fail them on the sixth."

When the old doctor had gone, Duncan paused uncertainly, a lump in his throat. He went into the kitchen, where Jean was doing her final tidying. She looked up and smiled at him.

"Your clothes are dry now. I'll have them pressed and ready for you in the morning."

"Thank you. You're—you're terribly kind, Miss Murdoch."

"Ooh," she chided him in the local dialect, "ye musna call me 'Miss Murdoch.' I'm just 'Jean.' But while I remember— here's a sprig of white heather. It fell out of your jacket pocket. I saved it for you in case it was for luck."

"It is indeed," he answered warmly, accepting it from her. "I wouldn't have lost that for the world."

"A keepsake?" she ventured.

"It's from the bonniest, finest girl in all the world."

"Does she love you—very much?"

He laughed, shaken out of his natural reticence. "When I've done something, made a name for myself, got the best practice in Edinburgh—maybe she will! In the meantime, it's enough that I—" He broke off.

"I'm glad," she murmured. "So glad for your sake. Someday I know she'll be very proud of you."

Overnight the rain cleared, the storm abated. Driven by Hamish, the doctor's man, Duncan left Linton at dawn. Like

24

most true natives of the glen, Hamish had a high suspicion of all strangers. A grunted, "Ye're for College, I'm told," was the limit of his conversation for the ninety-minute drive.

Duncan was glad enough to have the silence. The kindness of the night before had strangely sobered him. Yet as they rolled into the outskirts of the old, slate-roofed city by the sea, and the spired outline of the College buildings rose in gothic tracery against the eastern sky, he could not repress a quick, ecstatic thrill.

He wandered in a kind of heady rapture around the University precincts. Few students were about, since the term was not due to begin for another week. In its present solitude, the ancient structures, with their shadowed cloisters, their close-clipped sward and echoing quadrangles, had an air of grandeur and repose.

When nine o'clock chimed from the College clock, Duncan was brought abruptly to reality. Buttoning his coat, he thrust his chin out and started in the direction of the Dean's house. So imposing was this mansion, it made him hesitate; but he rang the bell resolutely, and a moment later was seated in the red-carpeted, richly furnished study. Here, twisting his cap upon his knee, he waited until the door swung open and Dr. Inglis entered.

Well?" the Dean inquired, and his expression was not encouraging. A precise little man with a tiny tuft of beard, gold pince-nez, and iron-gray hair meticulously parted in the middle, he had an air befitting the Chief Physician of the Victoria Hospital and the Chancellor of the great new Wallace Foundation in Edinburgh. But, despite his outward self-sufficiency, his eyes were mildly harassed.

On his feet, Duncan blurted out his purpose and his name.

"So!" The Dean sat down at his mahogany desk and waved Duncan to resume his chair. "I don't as a rule see students at this hour, but—" he picked up a paper before him—"only yesterday I had a letter about you from Colonel Scott."

CHAPTER 9

Duncan's heart leaped; yet before he could speak, the other continued, "While one is sympathetic to such aspirations as yours, it is my duty to warn you—"

"But Dr. Inglis—" Duncan interrupted.

The other raised his finger fussily. "Every year an army of ambitious youths invades this College. And every year we witness, my dear young sir, a massacre! In the Lockhart Examination only the most exceptional talent has a chance to achieve success. Think of it—among seven hundred candidates, three scholarships!"

"I have thought of it," Duncan said.

The Dean threw up his hands. "Then suppose you had the full opportunity, ample funds to qualify as a physician. Have you considered your physical limitations?" He gazed sympathetically at Duncan's arm. "Would you not be forced into some corner of the great profession, some obscure nook in, say, the public-health administration, where your lot would be the dusty office, the neglected desk?"

The Dean paused. "Forgive me, my dear sir, if I am frank. Reflect! Consider! Do not beat your head against the rocks of the inevitable! If circumstances make it impossible for you to return to your native town, out of regard for Colonel Scott I will find you a position in some subordinate capacity. I might even take you into my own household, where I understand from Mrs. Inglis—" his worried look deepened—"our domestic situation is temporarily somewhat strained, and we could make a place for a willing young man!" He concluded with a gesture and smiled kindly. "Well?" he asked.

Duncan got up abruptly. "Will you tell me where I register for the examination, please?"

To his credit, the Dean hid his discomfiture. "At the administration building, main block."

"Thank you, sir." Duncan turned and was about to leave the room.

In spite of his primness, there was kindness behind the Dean's starched shirt. "Here is a list of accredited student lodgings in the city." A spark of humor kindled in his eyes. "And may God have mercy on your soul!"

Duncan accepted the folder with a word of thanks.

After he left he felt a rush of obstinate resentment. Spurred by his indignation, he marched straight across to the registrar's and entered his name for the examination. He then set out to find a room.

At first he was unsuccessful. All the lodgings he viewed were too obnoxiously genteel or too obviously expensive. But at last, in the old quarter of the town close to the harbor, amid a litter of nets and tar barrels and the tang of salt, of herrings and the sea, he found in the narrow alleys where the fishermen lived, a low-browed house with an outside stair and in the window a notice, "Rooms."

At his knock, Mrs. Gait, the landlady, came. She contemplated him with a melancholy asperity, wiping her wet hands on her sacking apron—a wisp of a creature with an almost comic air of gloom. "Aye, I have got a room," she answered his inquiry. "It isn't much, and it's at the top of the house. But I'm only asking a pound a week."

He followed her into the house. The room was, as she had said, a small bit of a place; but it was clean, with a view of the ocean, the rooftops, and the College tower. He took the lodging on the spot, paid his twenty shillings in advance, and as the door closed behind Mrs. Gait, he began to unpack his books, reckoning what time he had to spend on them before the zero hour arrived.

CHAPTER 10

Only too soon it was upon him—that fatal Thursday morning. When he was seated at his desk in the University Great Hall, the strain of waiting, the intolerable suspense, made perspiration break out on the palms of his hands.

Rows upon rows of little varnished yellow desks, each like his own, each occupied by a candidate. Hundreds of young men, filling the Hall to overflowing, all ready to strive, to fight in competition with him. What chance had he among so many?

With an effort he focused his eyes on the high rostrum, where the two examiners sat. Fussing around them, in their gowns, were junior professors, lecturers, and senior scholars, among them Dr. Euen Overton.

Duncan had seen him as he entered the Hall, had received a vague and hypercritical nod of recognition, as though to say, "Please don't presume upon our previous acquaintance." How easy it would have been for Overton to have smiled, to have whispered: "Good luck, Stirling! Go in and win."

They were giving out the papers now. Nervously, Duncan picked up his pen. It was an agonized eternity before the first slip reached him: a composite examination on mathematics.

Yes, it was difficult. But not too difficult. At that he forgot everything, heard nothing of the rustle of papers, the scratching of the pens about him. His surroundings dissolved into blurred oblivion as he began to answer the first question.

At eleven o'clock the answers were taken in, the second examination was given out. Greek. Duncan had lost his nervousness now. Onward he went, in the feverish drive of his endeavor.

One o'clock brought the lunch recess. Duncan rose dizzily, followed others from the Hall. Most of the candidates went piling into the Students' Union, laughing and joking, exchanging comments.

While he stood on the steps, Overton approached, hesitated, then stopped.

"Feeling pretty lost, eh, Stirling?"

Duncan nodded, his eyes squarely on the other man.

"What solution did you get to that second trigonometry problem?"

Duncan gave his answer.

Overton's grin broadened condescendingly. "Yes, I thought you'd go wrong there! Too bad, isn't it? Well, I'm lunching with Dr. Inglis—I must rush!" With a nod he was off.

Duncan murmured to himself in a kind of secret agony, "O God, let me do something to show that I'm as good as he!"

Two o'clock brought the Latin examination. Then came English, followed by a half-hour respite.

Once again forgetting about food, Duncan chose a textbook from his bundle. The final examination of the day was yet to come, and it was history, his weakest subject. In desperation, he opened his book at random.

It was the chapter on the French Revolution he chanced upon, and, in particular, a full analysis of the part played in it by Robespierre. Flogging his tired mind, Duncan steadily read on until the final summons of the bell, then marched for the last time into the Hall.

The papers were distributed. The first, the major question on the sheet, was: "Write an essay on the character of the statesman, Robespierre." Duncan gave a gasp that held something of a sob, and began to write furiously.

Then it was over. Outside it was cool and dark, the street lamps making that starry spangle Duncan had always loved. He felt utterly exhausted, as though for hours he had poured out his strength in unavailing conflict.

He mounted the dark stairway to his lodging, threw off his clothes, flung himself into bed, and slept like the dead.

CHAPTER 11

Next morning he woke late, with a sense of languor. All day he wandered through the old town, watching the boats, the fish market, the gulls circling around the breakwater. He did not think of the examination or of the results, to be announced the following day.

The succeeding day he awakened with a premonition of disaster. He could not bring himself to approach the University; nor yet, perversely, could he keep away from it. Miserable, he hung about the forecourt, where there stood a huge bronze statue, memorial to Dr. John Hunter, world-famed physician and alumnus of this same College of St. Andrews.

Duncan's apprehension turned to hopelessness as he regarded the rugged old man. Suddenly he heard a voice at his elbow. One of the college janitors, inspecting him suspiciously, demanded to know why he was loitering.

Duncan started. "I'm waiting for the results of the Bursary Examination."

"They've been posted this last three hours!" the man remarked bluntly.

A shock ran through Duncan. How he reached the first flight of the office block, he never knew; but somehow he was there before the notice board.

For a full moment he could not lift his eyes to the small typewritten notice pinned up with brass drawing pins. He was like a man under sentence of death, knowing the reprieve is not there, refusing to meet the warden's gaze. But at last, with a desperate effort, he looked up.

The first name on that fatal slip of paper was not his. He had known it. A quick pain went through him. Nor, for that matter, was the second. That also had he known. But the third—his heart almost ceased its beating—the third name was his, "Duncan Stirling of Levenford."

He had done it! There was no mistake! There in red type-script was the evidence. The miracle had happened. He had won the Bursary!

As he found his way downstairs, a great emotion suffused him. Wildly, he thought of Margaret Scott. If only she were here! He must write to her at once. She would rejoice in his success! As he reached the statue of John Hunter, he halted momentarily and reached out his good right arm. "Now I'm on the way, John Hunter! I want to climb up there beside you!"

CHAPTER 12

Back at his lodging, he rushed into the kitchen. The first shock of unbelief was gone, supplanted by a surge of exultation. He must tell someone or he would burst. Seizing Mrs. Gait by the waist, he danced her around the room.

"I've done it, woman! I've won my Bursary!"

"For pity's sake!" She struggled. "Have ye gone crazy?"

"Don't you understand?" He whirled her off her feet. "I've got it! Enough to pay the fees of all my classes for the next five years! I'm going to be a doctor!"

"Let me go, you loon!" she laughed. "Or we'll both be needin' a doctor here this minute." She caught her breath as he released her. "While I remember, a big package has come for ye. It arrived just before ye came in."

"A package!" He was upstairs in a flash, and there was a great sacking parcel on the floor. Quickly he undid the string. Out tumbled a case of provisions, a sack of oatmeal, and a heavy bag of books—anatomy, surgery, medicine. On top of all was a note. He tore it open. It was dated that same afternoon from the doctor's house at Linton.

"Dear Professor:

"We've had our eye on you, and we heard the good news by phone even before you knew it yourself. Heaven knows, the examiners have made fools of themselves, letting such a dunce win one of the Bursaries. But mistakes will happen in the best-regulated universities. If you don't profit by this one, you're not the lad I think you are. Meanwhile, if you'll take an older man's advice, don't let them bamboozle you with any newfangled nonsense in the medical school. Keep your eye keen, mind your first principles, and use your good Scots common sense!

"At present we take the liberty of sending you, by Hamish, a few odds and ends to keep you in good heart. Also, here are some of my own textbooks. I never read them. They're not worth a docken. Don't get a swelled head, boy, and let us see you sometimes, you cross-grained, cantankerous, impossible Scot! God bless you."

"Murdoch."

The words misted under his gaze. He sat down on his bed, and for the second time that day his heart overflowed so that he could see no more.

CHAPTER 13

To Duncan, hastening from a late clinic to Dean Inglis's house, it seemed as though his college course had passed as swiftly as the whirling leaves. He was now a fifth-year student, and this coming winter would bring his final test. In a few short weeks he would be a doctor!

The struggle had left its mark upon him. At the beginning he had supported himself by clerical work at a local shop. In the end he had been forced to swallow his pride and accept the offer the Dean originally had made him. For three years now, after class hours, he had served in the Inglis home as houseboy. Inglis himself he had come to like. The little Dean had a shy, quizzical geniality beneath his protective shell of officiousness. But Mrs. Inglis was a mean, domineering woman, who drove him hard, and the wages were barely enough to pay his rent, to keep his body and soul together.

Arrived at the Dean's house, he went through the back door, substituted a blue-striped apron for his jacket, and began his usual routine chopping wood, filling scuttles, scrubbing the kitchen, stoking the furnace in the basement. He was in the kitchen when Mrs. Inglis came in. She was a full-bosomed woman, overdressed, aggressive.

"Stirling, I want a fire in the drawing room."

"Very well, Mrs. Inglis."

She gave him a hard stare. She disliked him. "Quickly! My niece is visiting me."

He was accustomed now to the petty humiliations she thrust upon him. Taking a scuttle of coal and kindling, he went into the drawing room. And there, seated on the couch with a book, was Margaret Scott.

At the sight of her he stood still, all the pent-up longing of his hungry heart bent upon her. For a moment she did not realize that it was he.

Then suddenly she cried, "Why, Duncan!" Bewilderment was supplanted by amusement, and her bright laugh rang out. At last she gasped, "Oh, forgive me, please, I didn't know you were the second housemaid!"

"First and second combined!" He had recovered himself by now. Giving her a quiet smile, he went forward and began to make the fire.

Head speculatively on one side, she tried to sum him up. "You've changed since I saw you last."

"There was room for improvement."

"Father was talking about you only the other day. He was having a discussion with Joe Overton about the big power plant they've started at last. Your name came up somehow. We scarcely ever see you."

The fire was burning briskly now. He stood up. A sudden reckless idea had been fostered by her lightly spoken remark. He said quickly: "It's quite true. I haven't seen you for ages, Margaret. Would you—would you come to tea tomorrow?"

She was frankly taken aback. "Where? At your rooms?"

He nodded.

She could not quite make him out. Yet she reflected that it might, after all, be fun to see this queer fellow at home. He had improved, for all this ridiculous position, beyond recognition.

"I can't come tomorrow," she said. "I'm going out with Dr. Overton."

He was silent. More than ever, Overton's name stirred in him a current of hostility. Since Duncan's success in the Lockhart Examination, the other man had gone out of his way to ignore him, or, on the rare occasions when they met, to treat him with exaggerated disdain.

"But I could—the following day," Margaret said.

Duncan was still glowing with happiness when he reached his lodgings that evening. Racing upstairs, he paused abruptly on the second flight. Someone was playing a piano. A new lodger, of whom Mrs. Gait had spoken, must have arrived. He stood in the shadow of the half landing, listening. It was really beautiful playing, quite outside his experience. Ordinarily he would have been too shy to take the step; but tonight his happiness overcame his reserve. He tapped on the door, and when a voice said, "Come in," he turned the handle.

"I happened to be passing—thought I'd better introduce myself. You're Dr. Geisler, aren't you? I'm Duncan Stirling—I live up above you."

Still playing, the woman at the piano turned her head and inspected him. She was about twenty-eight years old. Her eyes, darkly unhappy in her pale, rather ordinary face, had a curiously challenging quality. She wore a blue-and-white-striped cotton blouse, open at the neck, and a pair of dark-blue slacks. Her bare feet were in old red morocco slippers. Her black hair looked as unruly as her dress. He had never seen a woman so completely and so carelessly unfeminine. It was as though she had resolved on an utter lack of charm.

She reached the end of a phrase, stood up suddenly.

"Oh, yes," she said coolly. "The incomparable medical student! Mrs. Gait has been singing your praises ever since I arrived."

He laughed, then glanced around the room, which, though furnished simply, had an odd distinction: the one picture above the mantel—a splash of green and ochre—the couch covered in smooth cream satin, the small grand piano. It was surprising to find such pieces under this modest roof.

He could not help remarking: "You've made this attractive. Your own things, I suppose?"

Hardness returned to her face. "What remains of them."

He withdrew his gaze. He already knew that she was an Austrian refugee from Vienna who was coming to the University as a clinician in orthopedic surgery under the new medical-assistance scheme organized by the Council of the Wallace Foundation.

With cold cynicism she went on, "When one wants to get out of a country, one is glad to leave—anyhow."

"Yes," he agreed. "I daresay."

"I like this old house," she said after a moment. "It's so different from—the new Vienna." She shook her head as though to banish a memory. "Will my piano disturb you?"

"No, no," he said quickly. "I like it. That was a lovely tune you were playing as I came in."

"Tune?" she parodied, lifting her eyebrows a little. "Yes—that was Schumann, a dear little man. He died, like so many of them, in the madhouse." She threw back her head, eyes on the ceiling, features obscure, fingers moving gently across the keys. "Music! Dope! That's what this is to me. Come in and have some of it—any time, if you're not too busy. You needn't be afraid of me."

He was dismissed, abruptly and impersonally; yet somehow there was no sting behind her command.

"Good-night, Dr. Geisler," he said. "I hope we'll be friends."

Walking upstairs, he felt her music flowing after him in a strange, harmonious stream.

CHAPTER 14

The hour of Margaret's visit arrived. Duncan had borrowed from Mrs. Gait a new white cloth and a vase, in which he had placed some white roses. He had biscuits, cake, and a pot of strawberry jam for his guest. His budget, trimmed to the fraction of a farthing, had cracked beneath the burden of such luxuries. In desperation he had even gone to the pawnbroker's and pledged his father's watch and chain—a parting gift from the elder man.

As he stood viewing his preparations for the last time, Margaret's quick step sounded on the stair. A moment later she appeared, exquisite in a short mink jacket with a saucy cap and muff of the same rich fur. Her cheeks had a glow from the cold east wind; her eyes were sparkling with vivacity.

"What an odd little room!" she declared, lightly giving him her hand and surveying her surroundings with a comically wrinkled nose. "Is this really where you live? Why, Duncan, you couldn't swing a cat in it!"

"I haven't a cat to swing." He smiled happily.

Her presence lit up the room for him. As he poured tea and gave her a cup, he said with deep sincerity: "It's a great event, your coming here, Margaret. I cant tell you how much it means—" He broke off. "But I'm boring you. Have a piece of cake?"

"You don't bore me, Duncan. I love pretty speeches—when they're about me! But I can't, if you don't mind, touch the cake. Euen—Dr. Overton—gave me such a grim lecture on carbohydrates last night. Rather, when he was feeding me lobster and champagne! But you were saying something nice," she went on. "About me. What was it?"

"Oh, nothing."

"Please."

"Well," he hesitated. "It's just—I've always wanted to tell

you—what an inspiration you've been to me, all the years I've worked in this drab little place."

"You angel!" she exclaimed, pleased. "Give me another cup of tea and tell me all about it."

A glow went through him. His party was going better than he had dared to hope it would. He reached forward for her cup. As he began to fill it, a riotous knocking sounded on his door and a voice rang out, "Are ye at home, Duncan lad?"

There was a strained interval. Then he called, "Who is it?" But in his heart he already knew.

"It's your father come to see you."

CHAPTER 15

His father! The last person he had expected. As he rose constrainedly, the door was flung open, and Long Tom, followed by Rust, came staggering in. Long Tom was drunk, and deep affection for his son swam in his happy, full-moon face.

"How are ye, lad?" he fondly hiccoughed. "I had the chance to come over on a one-day bus trip. I couldn't resist it. For months past I've been weary to see ye!" Advancing, he folded Duncan in his arms. At that, Rust, in a delirium of greeting, leaped for his master.

Such pandemonium overtaxed the limits of the small room. A lurch from Long Tom and the vase of roses shattered on the floor.

"Save and preserve us!" Sobered slightly by the crash, Long Tom teetered around. "I didn't know ye had a visitor. By all the powers, it's yourself, Miss Margaret! I'm proud and pleased to meet you!" He held out his hand.

She ignored it stiffly.

"Sit down, Father." With torture in his eyes, Duncan took his father's arm and steered him to a chair. "You need a cup of tea."

"Tea?" Long Tom laughed jovially. "I know a better one than that." With a friendly wink at Margaret, he produced a bottle from his hip pocket. "Your good health, Miss."

"I'm afraid I must go now," said Margaret, beginning to draw on her gloves.

"Please." In his anguish Duncan entreated her to stay. "Father, try to drink the tea."

"I tell ye, I'm wantin' none of your tea, Duncan. I'd rather talk to your visitor."

Margaret got to her feet. "Dinna leave on my account," cried Long Tom, upset. To emphasize his protest, he tried to stop her with his arm. It was a fatal gesture. Striking the cup Duncan held, the old man sent a splash of tea over Margaret's coat.

A painful stillness filled the room. Margaret went white with temper and vexation. Duncan stood rooted in dismay.

"Oh, Margaret," he said. "I'm sorry."

"You should be!" she answered furiously. "I came here to drink tea, not to have it thrown at me by a drunken boor!"

What was there for him to say? Torn between two loyalties, he could only stand mute, wishing the floor would open and engulf him.

Perhaps she felt for him a little, yet even so her sarcasm was vixenish. "Thank you for a really charming evening. Everything was delightful!"

Then she was gone.

Long Tom, frowning and befuddled, took another drink to steady himself. He sighed. "Ye're not very pleased to see me, I'm thinking son."

"You know I am, Dad," Duncan hastily assured him. "It's just that—oh, what's the use?"

"Ye may well say, 'What's the use?' " The old man groaned. "Oh, Lord in Heaven, why did I ever come? I'm not wanted here. My own son's ashamed of me."

"Father," Duncan, patience ebbing, said fiercely, "it's time you slept this off!" He took the other's shoulder and helped him to the bed. Long Tom blinked at Duncan and yawned, tried to say something, abruptly was asleep.

Duncan studied the supine figure with a set, yet pitying face. Out of the turmoil in his heart came a sudden flash he'd got a fit reward, he thought, for pawning the old man's watch!

He made his father as comfortable as he could; then with a savage desire to forget, he left the room.

CHAPTER 16

The door below was open as he went downstairs; the voice of Dr. Geisler arrested him: "Is that you, Stirling? Stop in a moment."

"I'm going out," he answered roughly.

"Where?" Holding the skirt of the long gray robe she wore, she walked to the lighted doorway.

"I don't know."

Her expression did not alter. "Come in and keep me company."

Grudgingly, he entered.

"Quite a party you had upstairs," she said. "I saw the girl friend descend." She paused.

He laughed harshly and on an impulse etched the situation for her in a few acid strokes.

"Well, well," she commented. "Nothing for her to make a fuss about! Tell me, are you cross with your father?"

"No—just with myself. Probably my own clumsiness! What can you expect from a one-armed fool?"

"Come, don't be downhearted. It's not worth it."

She went to the piano. And while he sat before her warm fire, she played to him. First, as though touched by nostalgia, she played the lyrics, the waltzes of her beloved native city. Then she struck into Tchaikovsky's Fourth Symphony. Gradually, as the haunting harmony flooded the room, while the flames leaped and flickered, he felt a quietude steal over him. And when she had finished, he was at peace.

"Now do you want to run away?" she asked.

"No, confound you! I want to go on, do things—make my mark in medicine."

"So? You are interested in your work?"

"Terribly." He watched her as she approached. "You play beautifully."

"It is good for my fingers, makes them strong, supple."

She sat in her chair by the fire. "Don't forget, I am a surgeon."

He raised his head quickly. "I had almost forgotten," he admitted. And then went on: "Though, as a matter of fact your name has been in my mind. There's a very famous Dr. Geisler in Austria—Dr. Anna Geisler. Wrote a wonderful textbook on modern surgery. Are you a relative?"

"Not exactly." She lit a cigarette calmly. "I *am* Dr. Anna Geisler."

At first he thought she was joking. Then, as the very indifference of her attitude convinced him, he was stunned. She, the brilliant Geisler of Heidelberg and Vienna!

"Good Lord," he faltered. "Here I have been laying down the law, and you—your work is known the world over."

"You flatter me," she said.

"No, no. I'm just overwhelmed!"

She studied the glowing end of her cigarette. "It is nothing to what I have in preparation. When I am through here—with this little twelve months' job—the Commission, through your friend Dean Inglis, has promised me a great chance, in Edinburgh, at the Wallace Foundation! Then they will hear from me." She turned to him abruptly. "If you are doing nothing better, why not come and watch me operate tomorrow?"

"I'd like it above all things," he said eagerly.

She nodded, without further elaboration of the subject. Then she got up, trailed her robe across the room.

"I am hungry. And I am no cook, worse luck! But with the help of Hippocrates I am going to carve two noble sandwiches."

She did better than that, for she conjured up coffee and a jar of gherkins. They ate, seated on the hearth rug, talking of the technicalities of their trade. Her range of reading, the incisive force of her knowledge, amazed and deeply impressed him.

CHAPTER 17

When, at ten o'clock, he rose to take his leave, he said with gratitude: "This has been a most tremendous treat for me. I don't know how to thank you, Dr. Geisler."

She replied: "The name is 'Anna.' Don't try to thank me. If I'd been bored, I'd have put you out long ago."

When he had gone, she stood quietly, calculating. "Poor fool," she reflected, "he's been hurt by life. As I have been. But he hasn't hardened himself, as I have, yet." Standing by the dying embers, she thought, with brutal frankness: "I will take him in hand, and polish and harden him. He's clever. As a colleague, he may later on be useful to my work."

Next morning Duncan was wakened by a summons to the telephone downstairs. It was Margaret, prettily contrite for her tantrum.

He did not know that the thought of losing even the least of her admirers was wormwood to her vanity. No, it was a miracle for her to call him, to forgive him, to restore their relationship.

Long Tom, burdened by a headache and a deadlier remorse, received the news of the reconciliation with a groan of relief.

"Bungling old fool that I am! But I'll be punished—never fear! When I get home. I have your mother to face."

At the mention of his mother, Duncan's expression hardened. His estrangement from her persisted—strengthened on her part, rather than dissolved, by his attempts at reconciliation. She insisted even yet that all his efforts would end in tragedy, that time would prove her right.

He clenched his fist involuntarily. "Can you understand my ambition now, Dad? Why there must be no letdown? Why I must be successful?"

Long Tom's preparation for departure was now complete. He nodded as he pulled his cap on, made his way toward the door. "Be as successful as ye like, lad—but don't forget to be happy!"

He gave his son a final smile; then, calling Rust, he was off to catch the morning bus.

CHAPTER 18

That afternoon, Duncan set out to attend Dr. Geisler's operation. He arrived early at the little hospital, which was on a poor street in the manufacturing quarter of Dundee, a neighboring township. Yet Anna was there before him, washing up in the operating-room antechamber. Her manner was utterly impersonal. But as she was being helped into her gown by the operating-room nurse, she asked over her shoulder, "Would you care to give the anesthetic?"

Duncan was pleased and gratified. He began to thank her, but she cut him short.

"Please don't gush! Get ready," She turned to the nurse. "Nurse Dawson! I shall want my patient in just five minutes. Why isn't Dr. Overton here?"

Nurse Dawson, pert faced, with fluffy blonde hair and bold blue eyes, made an oddly self-conscious excuse. "He'll be here any minute now. I'm sure he's been terribly busy."

She had barely spoken when Overton hurried in, profusely explanatory for his delay. Duncan had anticipated the other man's presence, since it was Overton's duty, as one of the hospital's junior doctors, to assist. But, clearly, Overton had not expected him.

"Why, hello, Stirling!" A grudging admission lurked in the hostile greeting. "Didn't know you were today's ether merchant!"

"No conversation, please," Anna interrupted him sharply. "I never allow it in my operating theatre."

Overton shrugged his shoulders. But he made a sly grimace to pretty Nurse Dawson, as she helped him, solicitously, into his gown.

Almost immediately the patient was brought in—a boy eleven years old, underfed, wasted, a sack of bones and skin, a product of the surrounding slums. His was a case of talipes equines—club foot.

Like most children, he took the anesthetic naturally; Duncan, seated on the white metal stool at the head of the table, reassured by the deep and steady breathing of his charge, had a perfect vantage point from which to view the operation.

It looked like a hopeless condition—the shortened leg, the thickened and deformed foot, which was less a foot than a knob of twisted and deformed tissues. Duncan was convinced that not one surgeon in a thousand would have dreamed of attempting the operation. Yet he saw that, from her first swift and bold incision, circling the thickened ankle like a scarlet band, Anna was undertaking the impossible.

The thin-bladed lancet flashed unerringly in her cool, swift hands among the fuddle of bone and sinew. Every movement was direct and purposeful—nothing wasted, no fumbling, the intricate, fast moving fingers never at a loss. Duncan had seen fine surgeons at the hospital, the Regius Professor himself; but this was different, this was superlative, this unmistakably was genius.

When it was over at last, she turned away abruptly, peeled off her gloves, and with a long breath, walked into the alcove to remove her mask. There Duncan rejoined her. Overton was talking as he came in, and it was apparent that for once the young doctor had been moved from his habitual pose of boredom.

"Honestly, Dr. Geisler, that's the finest operation I've seen in the Infirmary. I congratulate you!"

She smiled distantly, drying her hands upon the towel he offered her. "Didn't I say, 'No foolish conversation'?"

"Then let's have tea." Ingratiating flattery was in his voice. "It's waiting for us both in the Common Room downstairs."

But his winning ways were lost on her. She shook her head. "I've already planned to have tea with a friend."

"Oh, well, another time, perhaps."

When he was gone, Anna made a grimace of distaste. "He is too handsome, that young man."

"He was genuinely enthusiastic about you."

"Perhaps. That type always has an ax to grind! Besides, I'll bet you a new stethoscope he's involved with that nurse." She discarded her operating gown. "But now, for heaven's sake, hurry up!"

"I thought you were going out with a friend."

"That's you."

As they were walking to the nearest cafe, she said: "You gave the ether well today. How'd you like to be my anesthetist for the next three months? The Infirmary allows me one. The fee is fifty guineas." He flushed with surprise and pleasure. Fifty guineas! It would end his penny pinching, his servitude to Mrs. Inglis—besides the distinction and experience involved.

Not looking at her, he said, "Are you really serious, Anna?"

She stared at him. "My good fellow, I am never anything else!"

CHAPTER 19

With a warm smile Duncan read the post card, typically unsigned, which bore the welcome and now familiar postmark of Strath Linton.

"Two ne'er-do-weel friends of yours will be in St. Andrews on Thursday afternoon. Meet them if you dare at Leckie's bookshop, one o'clock."

His friendship with Murdoch and Jean had ripened steadily, and on the rare occasions when the doctor and his daughter came to the city, he met them, before they all went on to lunch, at the bookstall. The old doctor, always on the lookout for a choice odd volume at a bargain price, made it his first port of call.

Suddenly, however, Duncan's smile faded. He had made an engagement for Thursday to take Anna to lunch in celebration of his new appointment.

Standing, card in hand, he had a vivid appreciation of all that the past six weeks had meant to him. In Anna Geisler he had found a colleague whose cynicism covered a purpose as deliberate as his own. Their association was extraordinarily impersonal, and this, to him, was its richest attribute. Under her influence, his studies had progressed, his ambitions deepened, his conception of surgery immeasurably widened. She lent him books, began to teach him something of art, of letters, of music. For all her brusque manner and careless appearance, she had a cultured mind.

He frowned at his dilemma. With an odd feeling of compunction he sat down and wrote a note to Murdoch, excusing himself on the grounds—since he had no wish to hurt his good friends' feelings—that he would be at work in the Infirmary on Thursday, which was, indeed, quite true, since he had an important session in the afternoon.

Thursday came. The luncheon was to be no hole-and-corner affair. He had decided to take Anna in style to the

Thistle Grill, one of the newest places in the city.

When he entered the Thistle lounge, she was already there. She was, today, less moody than usual. Her dress was black, extreme, and her black hat was a small felt absurdity with a scarlet quill. Never beautiful, she had a distinction of her own, with her colorless face, crimsoned lips, and lovely hands. She seemed, against the background of the provincial grill, sophisticated, out of place. Eyes were turned toward her—some interested, many primly disapproving.

The food was served, the wine uncorked, and Anna, leaning across the table, made him raise his glass to hers. "Prosit!" she declared. "To the medical future of Geisler and Stirling!"

CHAPTER 20

Something made him glance around. He started. Entering the restaurant were Dr. Murdoch and Jean. Both saw him instantly and, as they advanced, took in the close-up and clearly misread the momentary intimacy between Anna and himself.

Duncan colored deeply. It had never crossed his mind that Murdoch would choose this day to patronize the Thistle.

The old doctor, with Jean beside him, approached Duncan's table in passing to the end of the grill. As they reached him, Duncan half-rose, stammered an introduction, attempting to carry off the scene.

It was a ghastly failure. Murdoch, his shoulders hunched in his old tweed jacket, his gray brows drawn forbiddingly above his gimlet eyes, favored Anna with one comprehensive glare, then turned his back on her. Facing Duncan, he cleared his throat. "I see now why ye had no time for old friends today."

"But you don't understand—"

"I do!" Murdoch said scornfully. "Ye're working very hard at the Infirmary."

Trapped, through his stupid excuse, in something like a lie, Duncan sat down abruptly. Hurt and angry, he would say no more. Jean, with distress and misgiving on her face, started to speak. But Murdoch, a hand on her arm, was already stumping off with her to a far corner of the room.

After a moment's silence, Anna inquired, "Who is he?"

A particular friend of mine," Duncan answered stiffly.

"Oh!" Her brows went up. "And she?"

"The same!"

The careless camaraderie with which they had begun their meal was gone. Though they tried, Anna especially, to recapture it, Duncan was only too glad when the last tasteless course had been removed. Hurriedly he paid the bill and escorted Anna from the room.

They went straight to the Infirmary, where, at half-past two, Anna was due to operate—a major resection.

Today, partly because of the importance of the operation, partly because Anna's skill was now recognized, the theatre was crowded with students from the University, two local practitioners, a surgeon from the Victoria Hospital, and, to cap the list, a personage of first importance—old Professor Lee, head of the Wallace Foundation. Overton, always at his best when there was opportunity to show off, was assisting Anna.

When Duncan took his place at the head of the operating table, he was conscious of a vague misgiving. He was already upset by the incident at the restaurant, and the presence of so many spectators sent a wave of uneasiness over him. He had to give a difficult anesthetic—a mixture of gas, oxygen, and ether. He fumbled with his good hand among the complex taps and tubing.

As the operation proceeded, he knew that he was doing badly. Once or twice Anna looked at him sharply. Then he felt other glances, suddenly intercepted a critical stare directed by Dr. Overton toward his crippled arm.

All at once he was paralyzingly aware of his own deficiency. Stiff and awkward, he bungled the resetting of the three-way valve. His clumsiness increased, enveloping him like a fog, suffocating him.

And then, as he turned to renew the ether, the climax came. His fingers slipped, and he dropped the flask of anesthetic on the floor.

There was a shocked pause. All eyes were turned on Duncan, except Professor Lee's, which tactfully sought the ceiling.

"Clumsy idiot," muttered Overton. "Thank God, the cautery wasn't going. We'd all have been blown to blazes."

"Be quiet!" Anna snapped. She swung around to young Nurse Dawson. "Don't stand there like an idiot! Get another flask quick!"

"Yes, doctor." The nurse moved sulkily away.

The flask was brought, and the operation was tensely concluded.

CHAPTER 21

Duncan was pale as he went into the anteroom to change. He realized the enormity of his mistake, the frightful consequences that might have followed it. He felt weak and sick. He could not bring himself to face the others.

He delayed deliberately, waiting until Anna should have left the building. Then, as he was about to leave, he overheard the two surgical nurses outside—a mere snatch of conversation, but enough to arrest him like a blow.

"Wasn't it terrible," said the older nurse, "when that ether went? Awkward fellow!"

The other, Nurse Dawson, whom Anna had rebuked, answered crossly. "What can you expect? He'll never be any good as a doctor! Dr. Overton's told me that a dozen times."

Later, as he went home, the blackness of despair enveloped Duncan.

Next morning the mood persisted, a brooding darkness that overcast his soul. Never before had the cloud hung so heavily upon him. He became obsessed with the sense of his physical disability.

He fancied slights where none were intended, imagined his fellow students laughing at his wasted arm, became clumsier still through this perpetual morbid introspection.

On Saturday evening Anna stopped him on the stairs. "Young man!" She took him firmly by the lapels. "You've been avoiding me." She pulled him into her room. There she contemplated him. "What's the matter?"

"Nothing," he answered, his eyes averted.

She sat down, appeared to drop the subject. "You'll soon be having your final examinations," she remarked, in a purely conversational vein. "Next month, isn't it? I'm rather enjoying the thought of your getting through. You know, Duncan, if you gave yourself up to it—specialized—you and

I would make a wonderful team."

"Specialized in what? You know I'm fit for nothing!"

"Don't be absurd!"

Not heeding her, he went on tensely: "It's true. What am I good for? Inglis was right. When I started out, he warned me I'd end up in some cobwebby corner of the profession—a lame duck, working out vital statistics, splashing disinfectants down drains—it doesn't matter what. I'm not good for anything." He shrugged hopelessly.

The wound was open to her gaze at last. She said slowly, without a shade of sympathy in her voice, "If you'd let me get a word in edgewise, I'd point out how useful you could be."

He interrupted her savagely. "Don't let's delude ourselves. I'm a one-armed failure! God! I should have realized it long ago. When I began here five years ago, nothing seemed to matter but the fact that I could take my medical degree. I blinded myself to everything else. Now I see how futile it's all to be. No! Don't interrupt me. I may as well get it off my chest. How can I heal anyone? *How can I?*"

CHAPTER 22

Deliberately, Anna rose from her chair, and sat beside him. Her manner was entirely without emotion. "There's something I've wanted to ask you for a long time. This seems to be the appropriate moment." She looked straight into his eyes. "Will you let me see your arm?"

"Look if you wish," he said bitterly. "I don't mind. Walk up, ladies and gentlemen! A pin to see the peep show!" He began slowly to pull off his jacket.

She did not reply, apparently paid no heed as he loosened his collar and tie, stripped off his cotton shirt. But she could guess what agony it cost him to expose his deformity.

Naked to the waist, he faced her. She began her inspection with a blankly professional face. At first sight, despite her rigid control, she felt a tremor of dismay. As he had said, as she had feared, the condition was bad. The arm, fixed and contracted, had a withered look; like the dead branch of a tree.

"Move your fingers," she said.

He moved them slightly, with obvious effort.

"That's something," she commented, with sudden relief.

"What's the use?" he said dully. "It's all so hopeless. They've all seen it—Dr. Inglis, Tranton, Davidson. I even showed it to Professor Lee two years ago, at the Wallace Foundation."

"Will you keep quiet!" she cried sharply.

"All right." He eyed her bitterly. "Have your lesson in anatomy."

She began a manual examination, palpating the skin, the muscles, trying the stiffened joints, making him close his eyes while she tested cutaneous reaction with a needle point. Despite himself, he felt the latent power, the skill in every movement she made. It was a long time before she finished. Finally she said curtly, "Get dressed."

And then she said quietly, "Duncan, I want you to let me operate on that arm."

There was no mistaking the sincerity, the conviction in her words.

"But I tell you it's useless. I've had a dozen opinions. Professor Lee himself. He said an operation would be a deadly business, with little chance of amelioration."

"He was right in one thing." She spoke in the same monotone. "The operation would be a desperate affair. If I failed—" she paused—"you might lose your arm." Again she paused. "But I don't think I will fail."

He stared at her pale, emotionless face. A wave of doubts, of protest, of deep disbelief rose to his lips, then receded. He felt himself shivering, like a man who stands upon the brink of an abyss. Still watching her, he said, "Why do you want to do this thing?"

Her brows contracted. Her tone was strangely hushed. "Do you remember Pygmalion? Oh, I'm not thinking of you, but of myself. If I could accomplish this operation— this adventure in re-creation—not only would it better fit you to work with me, it would be my greatest triumph!"

His features relaxed; he smiled faintly, with ironic resolution. "Well," he said slowly, "in that case, put a good edge on your instruments. And if you see it isn't going the way you want it, slip the lancet in my jugular. I'm such a useless fool—I've a feeling I'd be better dead."

CHAPTER 23

Spring came early. The old gray city, leaping to life under its new green mantle, had never looked more lovely. Duncan walked down the High Street, afraid to hope that in a few short days he, too, might emerge regenerated and renewed. He entered the courtyard of the Infirmary.

To comply with the institution's regulations, he had to lodge certain forms with the registrar before he could be admitted. It was a mere formality. Yet his expression hardened as he approached the administration office. He knocked, went in.

Dr. Overton was tilted back in a swing chair behind his littered desk, his feet on the window sill. Perched on the arm of the chair close to him was Nurse Dawson.

Taken unaware, the nurse flushed, and a wave of confused annoyance colored Overton's brow.

"Oh! It's you, Stirling!"

As Nurse Dawson slid from the chair, tucking her hair beneath her cap, he turned to her with an assumption of authority. "That'll be all then, nurse. You can bring me those diet sheets later."

"Very good, doctor."

"Let me see now, Stirling," drawled Overton, without moving. "I did have those damned slips somewhere. You know, you're pretty lucky, getting that room in Anna's ward when we're so full up with important cases."

Duncan bit hard on his lip. "I'm quite aware of my insignificance."

"Oh, don't misunderstand me." Overton smiled with the old patronage. "It's just—you don't imagine for a minute she'll be able to do anything for that arm of yours!"

"No," said Duncan bitterly. "I'm only coming in here for a rest."

"Very funny! All the same, I've got to hand it to you, Stirling. You've made a regular hit with Anna Geisler. And she's a little lady who's going places. Believe me—" Overton grinned meaningly—"petticoat influence is an important thing!"

Duncan stiffened. There was something so underhand, so odious in the suggestion, he could have knocked Overton off his chair.

"Let's get through with this! I've a lot to do before I come in."

"No hurry, my dear fellow." Overton toyed irritatingly with a ruler. "You're ambitious, aren't you?"

"Aren't you?" Duncan asked.

"What d'you think?" Overton smiled again. "Wouldn't I get that from my father? You know he's started building his new hydroelectric works at Linton power and light for half the eastern counties. God, the old boy'll make a million! Well, I'm the same, Stirling. I've got to be recognized, talked about, right on the top."

Duncan's mouth was sardonic. "We're all green with envy at your job here."

"Good God!" Overton condescended to be amused. "This is just a springboard for my career. I go to the Victoria Hospital next, as subchief. Then I'm off to Edinburgh—to the Wallace Foundation!" He paused impressively. "Dr. Inglis is the big noise on the Committee there, and Mrs. Inglis is my very good friend. With my brains, influence, and connections, I lay you a fiver to a bob that within five years I'm the principal of that Foundation."

Duncan stared with dark, challenging eyes. He had a wild desire to accept the wager. But he merely said with chilly irony, "Nothing like aiming high."

"And watching where your feet go." Overton bounced the ruler on the desk and fumbled with the requisite forms. "Mostly mine go into the right drawing rooms. Back to the ladies again! And as you may have guessed when you barged in here, it isn't strictly business all the time. And I must say you made the trick with Anna. Well, put your name here. I'll see that you get the room."

CHAPTER 24

With the forms signed, Duncan left the office in a cold, dark fury. Overton's insolence, his smug, self-centered vanity, always maddened him. This cheap assumption involving Anna and himself was the final straw. He tried angrily to forget it.

But Overton did not forget. And Overton had a wide, malicious mouth. Before long the story of the proposed operation, suitably embellished, was broadcast through St. Andrews. It made a tasty meal for the scandalmongers. Two days later, Mrs. Inglis stopped Duncan as he swung past at midday from his clinic.

"I hear a great deal of talk," she said in a moral tone, "about Dr. Geisler and you. Is it true, what they say?"

"What do they say?" he countered bluntly.

She bridled confusedly. "You're always with her. In and out of her room at all hours, Dr. Overton told me."

"He keeps you supplied with the local lies."

She reddened. "He considers it his duty to inform me. I tell you straight—this won't do your career any good. I've talked to my husband about it."

He was furious, the more so since it now dawned on him he might perhaps have acted indiscreetly in his platonic relationship with Anna. And Mrs. Inglis, with the Dean under her thumb, was a woman who might do him serious harm.

In this mood, as he tramped down the High Street after the encounter, he saw in the distance a rugged, tweed-clad figure, bent over the stall of Leckie's Bookshop. His heart gave a bound, he forgot his worries and hastened his pace. It was the old doctor of Strath Linton.

"Murdoch! It's grand to see you again!"

Murdoch stiffened slightly, stared a little longer than was necessary at the open book in his hands, then briefly answered, "'Evening."

"I've been hoping I'd run into you," Duncan continued, "to explain about that unfortunate business—"

"I don't like explanations," Murdoch interrupted curtly. "And the least said about any unfortunate business—" he turned a page of the volume—"the soonest mended."

"But honestly," persisted Duncan, "You don't understand. I would have written. I was going to send a note to Jean—"

Murdoch turned and for the first time looked Duncan squarely in the face. He seemed older, somehow, his face more lined, his eyes more gauntly set; but his voice was hard as steel. "I wouldn't bother about that note if I were you. I'm rather particular with whom my daughter corresponds."

CHAPTER 25

There was no mistaking it. At the insult, Duncan flushed as though the old man had struck him.

So Murdoch had it, too! Duncan strove for self-control. Recollection of all that the other had done for him made him try to avoid a final parting.

"There's nothing but the best of friendship between Dr. Geisler and me. She's doing her utmost to put my arm right, staking her reputation on the operation."

"Staking her reputation is right," barked the older man.

Duncan could barely speak. "You're an old fool." He swallowed hard. "A prejudiced old fool!"

"Maybe I am!" growled Murdoch. "For I thought ye were a man once. I fancied ye had grit and spunk and good Scots gumption in ye. That's where I was a fool. Now I know ye're nothin' but a lapdog to a dolled-up foreign trollop! It's all over between you and me." Turning his back, the old man fumblingly picked up another book and eyed it fiercely.

Duncan could not see, in the gathering dusk, that Murdoch's fingers trembled so much he could scarcely hold the shaking pages. He knew only the hurt, the rankling injustice, in his own heart. Well, it was over now, that chapter in his history. Thenceforth he would erase Strath Linton from his life. He swung around and, without another word, walked rapidly down the darkening street.

On Thursday, two days later, he completed his final examinations. That same afternoon—a bright, fresh day, filled with hope and the promise of high summer, with big, fleecy clouds floating in the blue sky—he entered the room in Anna's ward for the operation.

CHAPTER 26

Six weeks later, lying in his narrow hospital room, Duncan feebly turned his head at the sound of footsteps in the corridor. His weakness was so extreme as to be absurd. Never had he dreamed what ravages the operation would effect upon his constitution.

He had been, they had told him, a full four hours on the operating table. For days afterward ether sickness had tormented him. And then the pain—it made him shudder—his whole left side a wall of living fire.

Anna had worked not only on the muscles, bones, and joints, but upon the plexus, that complex bunch of nerves, emerging with the great vessels from the armpit cavity. No opiate could fully ease the agony of those tortured nerves.

At night he had often prayed: "O God, now that I know the meaning of pain, now that I understand what suffering is, I'll be a better doctor, if I get through!"

The door opened quietly, and his nurse said: "A visitor for you, Mr. Stirling. She promises she won't stay long."

The next minute Jean stood in the doorway.

She brought a breath of the sweet hill country into the stuffy room. Against the reek of antiseptics rose a scent of pine and bog myrtle, of soap and woodsmoke. She came in shyly, in her simple brown dress, a beret carelessly upon her hair, parcels in her arms. There were diffidence and sharp anxiety in her warm young eyes.

"Jean!"

"Duncan!" she exclaimed. "You're awfully thin!" She went to his side.

"I'm awfully glad to see you, Jean. I thought you'd given me up for good." He stretched out his free hand—the other lay in boxlike plaster on the bed—and clasped her fingers tight.

"I was in town shopping. I had to come, even though you

63

and Father have had this dreadful quarrel."

Although he had resolved bitterly that all between Murdoch and himself was ended, he asked: "How is your dad?"

Her eyes clouded. "Not too well. He's out in all kinds of weather, you know, won't take care of himself. His bronchitis is bad. And then he's been so upset lately about the new dam they've started on Loch Linton, with a powerhouse and aluminum works and everything—great, smoking chimneys that will ruin the beauty of the glen."

He gazed at her troubled face. "A man named Overton's behind this scheme?"

She nodded. "Father has antagonized him already. I'm— I'm almost scared." She changed the subject hurriedly. "But I haven't come here to talk about Father and his troubles. Duncan, tell me! Is it going to be all right?"

He pressed her fingers again. "I'll know soon. They're taking off the cast today."

"Oh, I'm sure it'll be fine. I can't tell you—" she faltered—"every night I've lain awake thinking, hoping your arm would get well."

"You, at least—" he could not forego the remark— "approve of Dr. Geisler."

She faced him without flinching. "Anyone who does you good, Duncan, is good enough for me."

There was an awkward pause until Jean produced a gift of homemade jelly and scones she hoped he would enjoy. Then she gave him news of the Strath, of Hamish and their ancient car, of her new brood of chickens, the shooting party Sir John Aigle was planning for the twelfth, of Sir John's son, Alex, who had returned from Oxford to fight the unwelcome power scheme. Several times she protested she was tiring him and should go, and each time he insisted that she stay.

When at last she rose, he said, screwing up his eyes, "Jean, I'd have given anything to have had you for my sister."

She turned abruptly away. "Get better quick," she whispered. "That's all that matters, Duncan dear!"

Her visit heartened him beyond understanding.

CHAPTER 27

At three o'clock precisely, Dr. Geisler arrived with the head nurse to make her fateful visit.

"Well!" Anna exclaimed, seating herself on the edge of the bed and examining his bandages. "You seem actually to have a spot of color on your cheeks." She looked up from the wrappings and smiled at him. "Give me a chisel, nurse, please. Are you nervous?" she went on, and she began to chip the heavy cast delicately.

He moistened his dry lips. "You're the one who should be nervous."

"I don't suffer from that complaint," she retorted. "I've asked them to bring along the rheostat for your electrical reactions."

Faintness shook him as the plaster flakes fell away. It was happening so quickly now, this uncovering, after all that he had undergone. He had an impulse to ask them to put it off, to wait until tomorrow, before he learned the best or the worst.

But now the last of the plaster was removed and Anna began to release the under dressings. With a last, quick movement, the final gauze came off, and there, before his eyes, was his left arm.

At first he could not fully comprehend it, so fixed in his consciousness was the reality of a hunched and crooked limb. This was not hunched or crooked. Thin and limp though it was, it seemed now to be normal. Along its length the deep scars of the incisions ran lividly. The skin was bluish white. There it was, his recreated arm. She had broken and then remodeled it, as an artist might model clay.

"Well?" she inquired.

"I can see," he whispered unsteadily, "you've done a miraculous job."

"That remains to be seen," she replied crisply and signaled for the rheostat.

In a moment a nurse had wheeled the heavy electric machine alongside his bed. Aided by the other nurse, Anna adjusted the wires, dipped the pads in saline, and switched on the current.

A low whining filled the room. Propped up on his pillows, Duncan awaited the application of the terminals with an apprehension even greater than before. The success or failure of the operation swung in the balance of the next few seconds. He could hardly breathe as, one after another, the muscles of the reconditioned arm responded to the galvanic stimula. And then he knew, once and for all, that he was cured.

"We needn't worry now," Anna said. "You'll need weeks of massage and electricity. But believe me—" she spoke with dry derision—"you're as good as new."

"I know it," he said simply. "I can feel it—even now. Look!" Before anyone could restrain him, he made a quick effort and, raising his arm, took a glass from the stand.

"Don't!" cried the nurse in horror. "You'll do yourself harm!"

But Anna, watching intently, made a sign not to interfere.

They watched, fascinated, as he lifted the light medicine glass to his lips, drank from it, and placed it back on the table. Not since the paralysis had stricken him had such a movement been within his power.

"Well!" said the head nurse brusquely, relieving the tension of her own feelings. "After that, Mr. Stirling, I don't feel safe! In another minute you'll be throwing the furniture at us." She swung around before her subordinate could smile. "Come, nurse, help me take this apparatus out."

CHAPTER 28

When the two had gone, Anna and Duncan were silent.

"I owe so much to you," he said finally, with grave intensity. "From the beginning you've taught me about music, art, literature—you've educated me, you've civilized me. You found me a job when I most needed it. You've given me a wide, broad outlook in medicine. And now—" his voice fell—"this."

"For God's sake, Stirling! You Scots are such silly sentimentalists." She moved restively toward the window. "Haven't I told you that I have the satisfaction of achievement? I shall put you in my textbook—with dozens of illustrations and disgusting diagrams."

"Even so, you must let me say thank you, Anna. The most marvelous thing about it—in spite of all the gossip about us—is that you've done it in pure friendship."

"My dear Duncan," she broke in sharply, "must you go on like a professor of philosophy? Surely I deserve something better from you than that."

"I'm sorry, Anna," he said. "But I do feel so damned grateful to you. And there's so little I can do about it."

Fingering the curtain, she gazed out the window for a few moments. Then she said casually: "You can do quite a bit, Duncan. I'm not so altruistic as I look. I shall want you to work with me, help me with the pathological end of my research, pay me back that way." She turned quickly, her face pleasant, composed. "But we'll have plenty of time to fix that up later on. Meanwhile, it's just occurred to me—ten minutes ago your nurse made a horrible mistake."

"What?"

"She addressed you as Mr. Stirling. And since this morning the correct form of address is Dr. Stirling." She smiled as she went toward the door. "I had word from Dr. Inglis as I came up. He was quite excited. You've passed, Duncan, got your degree. With honors, too." She opened the door and, with a last look at his astonished face, rapidly went out.

He lay there motionless, wishing that he had called her back, thanked her more adequately. Then gradually the realization of his future broke upon him. Unconsciously he moved his liberated arm, clenched and unclenched the once-useless fist. A surge of power went through him. Now, at last, as Anna had said, the world was at his feet.

Suddenly he turned onto his elbow, took his worn old pocket book from the bedside table. From it he drew a snapshot, a sprig of faded heather. The snapshot was of Margaret; the heather was the token she had given him so long ago. She was away on holiday, at present, in Switzerland. "But now," he thought fervently, "I have something to offer her when she returns."

CHAPTER 29

On a fine morning toward the end of July, Duncan stood, white-coated and impatient, outside the Inglis ward of the Victoria Hospital, waiting for Euen Overton.

Six weeks before, on his leaving the Infirmary, Dean Inglis had made him house physician for his ward, the largest in the Victoria.

"I always believed in you, my dear Stirling." The worthy Dean, whose pessimism had almost annihilated Duncan's early hopes, had patted him benignly on the back. "And between ourselves," he had chuckled, "I want to indicate that belief in the face of sundry public and—er—private dissuasions." And taking Duncan's arm, he had led him along the hospital corridor to his lavishly equipped test room.

Duncan had moved into his quarters at the big hospital and, rejoicing in the strength of two sound hands, had thrown himself into the work he had longed for.

His days were full. He rose at seven and until breakfast was busy writing up his casebooks. The forenoon was occupied accompanying Dean Inglis on his official visit to the wards—an exercise in patience, since Inglis was slow to the point of distraction. After his hurried lunch, a protracted series of biochemical tests carried him on till six. The climax was an evening round with Overton, now the subchief of the hospital and ready to exert his new authority on the slightest provocation.

After six exhaustive weeks, a queer dissatisfaction tinged Duncan's ardor. He did not mind the tedium of his routine or the petty manifestations of Overton's spite; but at every turn he found himself frustrated in his burning desire to establish real contact with the sick.

A step in the vestibule made him look up. It was Overton. He waited till the other doctor drew near.

"Overton! I'd like to talk to you about that Walters case."

"What Walters case? I'm busy—on my way to breakfast."

"This is important, Overton. The young fellow in Bed 7—obscure chest symptoms. He's much worse."

"How the devil can I help it?" Overton had been out late at a dance the night before, with Nurse Dawson of the Infirmary, and for more reasons than one connected with the pretty nurse, he was in a bad temper. "We've done everything we can."

"Everything but find out what's wrong with him." Duncan's tone was hard. "I've done dozens of useless tests every day for a week, until I'm dizzy. Meanwhile, he's dying."

"The diagnosis is in doubt," Overton snapped. "We can't act. The Chief thinks it's an obscure anemia."

"In my opinion it's a plain, straightforward empyema. That man's chest should be tapped. If it isn't, he'll die."

"And who asked your opinion? Remember your position here, Stirling. It's only a fad of the Dean's that got you in. And a hell of a lot of people think you should be out."

He strode off down the corridor. Duncan, with a set and drawn face, watched him go.

CHAPTER 30

That evening he had an hour off duty. He spent it, as he usually did, in Anna's room. It gave him a wry pleasure to defy the current tattle of the town.

After she had given him coffee, she commented on his unusual silence. "What's the matter? Someone else gossiping about us?"

He shook his head. "No, I'm enjoying my introduction to mechanized medicine. It's amusing," he continued ironically, "to fuss with test tubes and basal metabolisms when, by putting my ear to a sick man's chest, I can tell in two minutes what's ailing him."

She looked at him closely. "Don't belittle the weapons of modern medicine, Duncan."

He suddenly broke loose. "For six weeks it's been growing on me! I want to work with my hands, not with gadgets—they're paralyzing the profession. Doctors tainted by money are only half the story. The other half is that doctors under our present system are being deprived of the qualities that really matter—personality, the capacity to inspire faith, the power to make a real diagnosis. They're never allowed to do anything themselves. There's always a nurse or a sister or a clinical clerk or a machine to do it for them. Right now there's a man dying in my ward because they can't see the truth for a forest of charts, graphs, calculations, and tests!"

Her silence was coldly disapproving. "It's time you cultivated a scientific approach to your work."

"And dropped the human one?" he shot back angrily.

"Why not? You'll find it little use—when you move on to pathology."

Brought up short, he stared at her.

Her gaze was as level as his own. "You're well aware we're going to team together. I shall want a really expert pathologist for my work on neuromuscular coordination."

"Your work," he said.

"Let's say our work. Don't forget you're quite definitely pledged to me." She smiled at him enigmatically, changed the subject lightly. "Relax now. I'll play you some Bach."

She had not solved his difficulty. She had created another.

He rose before his hour was up and went straight back to the ward. Opposite Bed 7 he stopped.

The patient, Walters, a young fellow of twenty-two, was in a desperate condition—lips parched, eyes dim, breathing shallow and distressed. In the subdued light of the ward, Duncan's frown grew deeper. He slipped his hand beneath the patient's bedjacket, sensing, with that secret faculty of touch, the deep-seated trouble beneath the heaving ribs.

He turned swiftly, beckoned the ward nurse to the bed. "I'd like the screens for this case, nurse. Will you bring them?"

In five minutes she was back with them. Accompanying her came a nurse and two probationers, bearing a blood-count apparatus, slides, covers, sterilizers, a trolley of reagents and stains, all paraphernalia of the higher ritual.

Duncan said curtly: "All I wanted, nurse, was a needle. Hand it to me, please."

He was bending over the patient when the sudden swish of the swinging door made him raise his head. Dr. Overton was entering the ward on his night visit.

"What's the meaning of this?" Though suppressed, Overton's voice was venomous.

Duncan straightened. "If you wait a moment, you'll see."

Overton flushed. "Are you out of your senses? You can't interfere with this patient without my permission."

"Must I have your permission to save his life?"

A shocked and startled hush had fallen on the attendant nurses. The sick man, straining his eyes from Overton's livid face to Duncan's hard, cold gaze, now feebly plucked at the younger doctor's sleeve.

"Go ahead, doctor," he gasped. "For pity's sake, do what you can to get me right."

"I warn you—" Overton's voice rose. "It's at your own risk!"

Defiantly, Duncan stooped again. He grasped the stylet firmly. His pulse was hammering as he plunged the instrument into the patient's chest. After an instant of suspense, the thick, yellow pus welled out through the puncture from the abscess in the pleura, as though it would never stop.

Walters sighed with relief. Overton was pale, and there were beads of sweat on his forehead. Wiping the instrument on a strand of gauze, Duncan spoke quietly to the sister.

"You'll have him removed to Ward E tonight, sister. He'll do famously with a rib resection."

"I'm doing famously already!" Tears of relief were running down young Walters' cheeks. "I can breathe proper now. God bless you, doctor!"

CHAPTER 31

Next morning, during their round, Duncan caught Dr. Inglis glancing at him oddly. When they were alone, the Dean buttonholed him nervously. After hemming and hawing for a moment, he remarked: "You don't get on well with Dr. Overton, Stirling."

"No, sir."

The Dean's features relaxed. He laughed. "Neither do I!" He collected himself, went on with his usual harassed diffidence. "All the same, my dear Stirling, I wish you hadn't upset your colleague. I needn't tell you there are forces against you here. Trouble may be in store for you. I sincerely trust not. But, I beg of you, in future be more orthodox."

Walters made an excellent recovery. Later, as Duncan discharged the grateful man, he could not repress the stubborn thought: "If I'd been orthodox, this nice youngster would be dead."

One Friday afternoon in late September, as Duncan stood in the test room, his work there almost finished for the day, a light knock sounded on the door. Before he could say, "Come in," Margaret stood beside him.

"You see!" she declared. "The mountain comes to Dr. Mahomet!"

"Margaret!" he said eagerly. "I'd no idea you were back!"

"Father had to dash home on business ten days ago—the new power company."

He said slowly, "It was nice of you to come to see me."

"Oh!" She laughed carelessly. "I had a message for Uncle Inglis, and I thought I'd drop in."

Her gaze had been appraising, as only Margaret's could appraise, his tall, straight, white-coated figure.

A sudden surge of longing overcame him. He had missed her dreadfully, awaited her return with growing impatience.

No longer now was he at a loss for words. Nor was he a struggling cripple with small hope of ultimate success. He knew, with stark conviction, that his ambition could take him to the heights.

CHAPTER 32

"Margaret," he said, "there's something I want to tell you."

She glanced up at his tone, round-eyed, teasing. "Well, so long as it isn't the story of your life!"

He took a step nearer her. "No, but it does go back quite a long way, Margaret. Back to a poor boy—and a princess who lived high up in her tower."

She looked up at him archly. "What nice things you say! Who was your princess?"

"Margaret, can't you guess?"

"You mean me?"

His answer was to take the faded sprig of heather from his wallet. "Don't you remember when you gave me this?"

"No." She shook her head, puzzled.

"By the river," he prompted. "That day I was fishing, and saw you."

"Why, yes. And you've kept it all these years?"

He nodded.

Caution almost halted her, yet still she warmed her vanity at the fire of his love. "I can't tell you how flattered I am."

He took her hand. "Margaret, I've waited so terribly long to be able to tell you this. I love you. I know I can make a great success of myself. And it'll all be for you, Margaret!" He rushed on blindly. "Will you marry me—when I've made my name, when I've made a place in the world for you and me?"

For as long as she could, she held his gaze. Then she gave a short sigh. Her eyes fell. "I shouldn't have let you go on," she murmured, with well-simulated confusion. "But I am fond of you—truly I am—and I did want to hear what you had to say."

"Why shouldn't you hear it?" he asked.

She released her hand slowly. "Well, you ought really to

have seen—"

She extended her left hand, displaying a large, new diamond on her engagement finger. "I'm surprised you didn't notice it. It's so huge—and such a beauty!"

He was stunned. He said slowly, heavily, "I'm stupid at these things, Margaret." There was a long pause. "It is a lovely ring." Again he paused, struggling for the words. "Who—who is he?"

He knew her answer before it came. "Why, Euen—Dr. Overton, of course. We've always been keen on each other. That's why I came to see you. To ask your congratulations. To have you wish me luck!"

With a tremendous effort, he kept the bitterness from his voice. "I do wish you luck, Margaret, and happiness—with all my heart."

"You must admit," she ran on, "it's a suitable match in every way. We have so many things in common. And Euen's new post at the Wallace Foundation will take us to Edinburgh. Father has promised us a darling house. You see, everyone seems to think that, in a few years, Euen is a safe bet for the principalship."

"You'll be married almost at once?"

She nodded. "Next month. You must come and dance at the wedding. I'm asking all my old admirers. Isn't it fun?"

Her flippancy evoked in him a flash of insight. For a moment he glimpsed the triviality of her mind. But it was gone, instantly, and in a tone of quiet sincerity he said, "If there's anything I can do, at any time, you've only to let me know."

She pressed his arm lightly, was about to answer, when the sound of a motor horn sent her flying to the window.

"That's Euen! We're playing golf before tea."

She swung around gaily, extended her hand with a vague compunction. "Good-bye. Don't bother to come down. We must rush, or the light'll be gone."

He stood at the window until they had driven off, steeling himself to watch the triumph in Overton's smile, the possessive fondness with which he handed Margaret into the car.

CHAPTER 33

Duncan had arranged to accompany Anna that evening to a concert given by the Philharmonic Orchestra. But now he called up Mrs. Gait and left word that he must cancel the engagement.

Toward half past ten, however, Anna marched into his room unannounced. She threw off her hat and flung herself into a chair. Then, without paying any heed to him, she picked up a local paper and began to read it.

He roused himself to ask, "Concert any good?"

"I didn't get there, either." Her manner was charged with a curious significance. "Don't be polite on my behalf. Continue the sitz bath of misery."

Ignoring his angry stare, she went on unperturbed: "Listen to the local organ of news and public thought—'Their many friends in St. Andrews society will learn with the greatest interest of the betrothal of Miss Margaret Scott and Dr. Euen Overton, announced by Mrs. Inglis, aunt of Miss Scott, last night. Miss Scott, well known for her activities amongst the younger fashionable set, is, of course, the daughter of Colonel John Scott of Stinchar Lodge.'"

She dropped the paper in disgust. "It makes me sick. You never loved that girl! You were in love with an ideal. You put her on a pedestal and went on your knees to worship her. Everywhere it's the same. In my country, every woodcutter's son makes his dream around the daughter of the *schloss.*"

He glared at her, but she went on: "She's nothing but a vain, selfish, empty-headed little flirt. How do you think you could have worked—with her, her perpetual demands, her stupid parties, her social strivings—"

"Anna!" Duncan jumped up, livid with anger.

"I know! I know!" she waved him aside carelessly. "If I had not operated on your arm, you would kill me where I sit. And if I didn't think you had some good in you, buried away beneath that sentimental hide, I would get up and walk out on you forever."

He gazed at her helplessly before he dropped back into his chair.

"That's better," she went on in an altered voice. "I know you are hurt. I know how it feels that she has chosen Overton." A slow, cynical smile crept over her face. "Don't you worry. He won't be so happy. Nor will she."

"Anna, be quiet!" He pressed his head into his hands.

She said with deliberation, "Nurse Dawson tried to commit suicide this evening."

"What?" he glanced up, bewildered. Then the meaning of it struck him like a blow.

Anna nodded. "A bungling, messy little affair. Can you imagine a trained nurse choosing an infirmary in which to swallow fifty sleeping tablets? We pumped her stomach clean as a whistle. It's all hushed up. She's been packed off to her people in Perth now, perfectly recovered, but—not quite so good as new."

Duncan stared at her.

"After the mix-up, her room was naturally chaotic. But I saw these—and thought it worth while to hang on to them."

She tossed him a bundle of letters. Slowly he untied them. They were from Overton. It took no more than a few minutes to reveal their purport.

"Yes," she remarked, as he raised his eyes to hers. "We have your dear, kind friend right over the well. It's going to be pleasant watching him fall in."

"No!"

"Why not? He's asked for it, spreading those lies about us—this paragon who seduces his own nurses!"

He shook his head sternly. "I couldn't, Anna! Never! It would hurt Margaret too much. I'll fight Overton, but not like that."

CHAPTER 34

She studied him with narrowed eyes, skillfully changed her ground. "Perhaps you're right. I've longed to see you really buckle down to beat that man. And now I think I know how you can do it. When do you finish at the Victoria?"

"The second week in October—if I'm not kicked out before."

"Splendid! On the fourteenth of October, go away for a change. A good, clean breeze, my friend, will blow this infatuation out of your head. In four short weeks I guarantee you will be cured. And then—"

"What?"

"Then I shall be ready for you."

"Ready for me?"

"The Commission proposes to move me to Edinburgh—not official yet, but practically settled. I shall have a major hospital appointment with full facilities at the Wallace Foundation. Also—" she added casually—"the choice of a colleague to assist me in pathological research."

His face was set, almost forbidding. "Pathology! The mortuary slab—God! I hate it."

"Don't be absurd! I have influence with the Commission. I may even get you the Pathology Chair. Head of department, at your age—think of it! And think what Overton will think of it!"

"Damn it! Why do you bring out the very worst in me?" he demanded.

"Because you're very much my property." She smiled sweetly. "Dear old Duncan. Now, more than ever."

"You are the most selfish, the most infernal woman I have ever met."

She stifled a yawn, looked at her watch. "Yes, where science is concerned, I am. And we're both marching under that banner." She threw him a last cool glance. "Sleep well, little woodcutter, your calf-love days are over."

As she moved to the door, she picked up the bundle of letters. Later, when she reached home, she sealed the package carefully and, with a strange smile, locked it away in a bureau drawer.

CHAPTER 35

Feverish and uncertain, tormented by the endless conflict in his mind, Duncan reached his last week at the Victoria Hospital.

The weather had become bitter cold, with sharp flurries of snow and a hard black frost that turned the ground to iron. Late one night, as he returned from his final round, the phone rang in his sitting room. Fancying it a belated call from Nurse Grant, he picked up the receiver mechanically.

It was not Nurse Grant. The voice came distantly, over miles of country wires. He realized with a start that it was Jean Murdoch.

"It's Father—he's laid up."

"What's the trouble?"

"It's bronchitis. We've had deep snow up here. Three nights running he was called up the Strath while he had a heavy cold. He just wouldn't give in—but now he has to."

"How about the practice?"

"That's what's bothering me. There's a lot of illness here."

He visualized the situation in lonely Strath Linton: the sick doctor, the icebound countryside, the widely scattered patients. "You need a substitute?"

"Indeed we do, at once. You wouldn't know of anybody?" She hesitated, then asked with a rush, "Oh, Duncan, you wouldn't be able to come up for a week or two yourself?"

He had already made his decision. Indeed, but for his estrangement from Murdoch, he would have offered his help before she asked it. He reflected quickly. In such an emergency Dean Inglis would, he felt sure, release him from this last few days at the Victoria. He said to Jean, "What time does the last bus leave?"

"Nine o'clock, from the Old Square."

"I can just about do it. Expect me at your place about ten o'clock."

He hung up the receiver, and put through a call to Dr. Inglis. Succinct and forceful explanation set him free. He had no time to pack a bag. He flung on scarf and overcoat, pulled his hat over his eyes, bolted downstairs. He sprinted along the deserted street and swung aboard the rickety country omnibus just as it was pulling out of the Old Square.

Usually the bus was crowded; but tonight only two other passengers were aboard—the first, a young fellow of twenty-five, with a clean-cut, well-bred face, who sat engrossed in a novel; the second, his immediate neighbor, caused Duncan an abrupt shock of recognition. Though he had not seen him for six years, there was no mistaking the full-bodied, heavy-jowled, middle-aged man, a trifle puffy beneath the eyes, his sparse black hair oiled across his forehead. It was Honest Joe Overton!

The older man soon made it plain that he had not forgotten Duncan. "It's you!" he growled. "What d'you want here on a night like this?"

"What do you?" retorted Duncan.

"Me!" grunted Honest Joe. "I've been visiting my son. I wouldn't be in this damned hearse if my car hadn't given out. Ignition trouble. Wait till I get hold of my mechanic— I'll wring his blasted neck." He pulled a cigar from his pocket, bit off the end, and asked as he lit up, "Going far?"

"Strath Linton," said Duncan.

"Ah!" said the other with a flash of interest. "The lovely glen! I'm hanging out not far from that Godforsaken spot, myself. Busy on the biggest project of my life, on Loch Linton—dam, sluices, turbines, generators, the whole bag of tricks, employing over a thousand men. All your friends in the Levenford Council are in with me. When we're through, we'll supply power and light to half the eastern counties. Practically a monopoly, besides running our own aluminum works to the bargain."

Duncan was silent. Besides what Jean had told him, there

had been much in the press lately. A violent controversy centered on the new scheme, which, while of unquestionable utility, would destroy the most famous beauty spot for miles around.

CHAPTER 36

You see that young upstart over there?" Honest Joe indicated their absorbed fellow traveler. "That's Alex Aigle, son of Sir John Aigle. By God, you wouldn't believe the trouble they've given us, those ruddy Aigles—trying to spike our scheme and save their picture-postcard property. But I've licked 'em!" He rubbed his hands together, then cocked his shifty eye at Duncan. "What, if I might be so bold, is your business in the valley of Linton?"

Duncan replied curtly, "I'm going up to fill in for the local man, Dr. Murdoch."

"Murdoch!" exclaimed the other vehemently. "That stiff-necked old swine!"

Duncan said coldly, "You know Dr. Murdoch?"

"Too well," growled the other. "I asked him to do me a favor on some compensation cases. A bunch of my men were fool enough to get enteric—started claiming sick benefit. Instead of helping me out, that old devil blamed the grub I was feeding them, swore he'd produce evidence in court if I didn't pay them."

"And of course he was wrong?" Duncan inquired evenly.

The contractor threw him a sharp look. "Right or wrong, I shan't forget your Dr. Murdoch in a hurry. Tell him that, from Joe Overton, when you see him. I'm glad he's sick— it's high time he died. They need a new, up-to-date young surgeon in Linton—and maybe I'm the man to bring him in."

"You'll be wasting your time," said Duncan coldly. "Every soul in the Strath loves old Murdoch." Turning his shoulder, he pulled a textbook from his pocket and began to read. As he did so, he thought he caught a half-smile of approval on young Aigle's face.

Though he tried to focus his thoughts upon his book, he was glad to reach the end of the long, cold journey. He strode through the quiet whiteness of the village, with the dry snow squeaking beneath his feet and the frost turning his breath to rime. A sense of exhilaration filled him; he was like a schoolboy coming home.

At the end of the road, the lights of the doctor's house gleamed into the night. He stamped his feet on the steps, lifted the heavy knocker; but before he could let it fall, the door was flung open and there was Jean, silhouetted against the warm brightness.

"Come in," she cried. "Oh, I'm glad to see you! It was fine of you to come!"

Quickly, eagerly, she helped him out of his coat, her eyes alight with the pleasure of seeing him again.

"And your arm," she said in a low voice. "Isn't it wonderful?" No more than that. But the gladness in her voice touched him like a living thing.

"Not so wonderful as your welcome, Jean." He stood gazing at her, reluctant to leave the warm comfort of her presence. Where's the invalid?"

"Upstairs. In an awful temper—which shows he's not so sick."

"I'll take a look at him right away, in any case." He smiled at her again and turned slowly toward the stairs.

The old doctor sat propped up on pillows in a high-backed chair, a rug about his knees, an asthma kettle puffing at his elbow. His cheeks were congested, his brow was flushed; yet out of his rheumy eyes he glowered at Duncan with indomitable wrath.

CHAPTER 37

"So," he wheezed, "it's the great man, himself. Straight from his test tubes and his braw white coats!"

Duncan glared back, with compound interest. "You ought to be in bed," he said curtly. "Your temperature's probably a hundred, and you're badly cyanosed."

"Cyanosed!" mimicked Murdoch. "That'll be one of your new scientific terms, God bless my soul! I'm almost cured already for the hearin' of it!"

"Please don't. You're making yourself worse!"

"Maybe I am," Murdoch spluttered. "But I'll get myself well, dear professor, without any high-falutin' help from you. I didna send for ye—it was Jean's will. And if ye dare to put one drop of your newfangled nonsense near me, I'll rise off this chair o' sickness and fell ye to the earth!" He paused, then added, with taunting irony, "But I near forgot—how is your fancy woman?"

Duncan gritted his teeth. "She's very well."

Murdoch bellowed: "You have disappointed me, you brazen young whelp. You should be ashamed of yourself!"

"And so should you, you stubborn old fool!" Then, since the scene was upsetting the sick man, Duncan made a great effort and controlled his bitter exasperation. "Will you let me have tomorrow's visiting list?" he said flatly.

Murdoch growled, "Jean'll let you have the list."

"Thank you." Duncan turned to go.

"There's an ill woman up at Blain Dhu," Murdoch said. "McKelvie's, the keeper's, wife. She's dying, poor body, of double pneumonia. It would be too much, on a night like this, to ask a la-de-da scientist to take a look at her." He averted his gaze. "But a man might want to go."

"Where is Blain Dhu?"

"A matter of fifteen miles up the mountain. Hamish knows the cottage." Murdoch paused, slowly raised his eyes.

"D'ye mean ye'll go?"

Duncan simply looked at him.

"Mind ye," Murdoch wheezed relentlessly, "ye'll do no good. But at least 'twill satisfy the husband. Don't be trying fancy treatments at the deathbed. Or McKelvie's like to brain ye where ye stand."

"I'll try what treatments I like," Duncan shot over his shoulder. "And be damned to McKelvie—and you!"

He slammed the door.

Downstairs he went into the little bare dispensary—pathetic, almost, with its wooden shelves, its few bottles, its tarnished brass scales. There he picked up Murdoch's bag—small, stained, and worn, the hasps yellowed, the black leather so weather-stained it had in patches turned rusty brown. Within, in meticulous arrangement, were the simplest drugs, the surest and best-tried implements of healing—a hypodermic, strychnine, morphine, a pair of old-fashioned midwifery forceps, a tourniquet, ligatures, needles, such a primitive armory, in fact, as might have served for Galen, or the master Hippocrates himself.

With a queer pang, Duncan carried the bag out to the car, took his seat beside Hamish. They drove off. If anything, the snow had thickened. It lay in great high banks where the snowplow had been at work. Presently, when they swung off the main thoroughfare onto a narrower hill road, the car began to plunge and flounder. All around the shrouded pine trees rose like specters.

Higher they climbed and still higher. Sharp gusts of wind caught them on the curves, drowning the whine of the windshield wiper and the crunch of the tire chains on the snow.

It was a solid hour before Hamish steered the car alongside the dim shape of a hut. Clearly they were expected. At once the door swung open.

After the whirling maze of whiteness thrown up by the headlights' glare, the lamplit interior seemed unnaturally dim. Blinking, Duncan made out the tall, strong figure of the gamekeeper—a young man under thirty, his face haggard with anxiety. By the stone hearth of the fireside stood an older woman, whom Duncan judged to be a neighbor, with two silent children beside her. The eyes of the four people were bent upon him with mute intensity and a strained distrust.

CHAPTER 38

"Dr. Murdoch's ill," Duncan said. "I am Dr. Stirling."

"Poor Annie!" The forester sank into a low wooden chair and buried his head in his hands.

At the sight of their father's distress the two children began to cry. The woman drew them to her, soothing them in a mournful undertone. "Dinna cry, my poor bairns—though you're good as motherless now."

Duncan fought back his dismay at such a reception, on such a night. In a recess at the far end of the room he heard labored breathing. He placed Murdoch's bag on the table and advanced toward the low box bed, where the patient lay.

One glance assured him of the diagnosis, the gravity of the case. No need here for all the scientific paraphernalia of his recent work. This patient, a young countrywoman, still beautiful despite the ravages of the infection, had lobar pneumonia of both lungs. And she was dying.

A great emotion rose in him. It was an instinct to battle, intoxicating, irresistible. With the urge to fight came a sense of power that flowed through all his being. This woman might be dying, yet she was still alive. And he would not, he must not let her die.

He took off his coat, rolled up his shirt sleeves, spoke to the neighbor woman by the fire. "I shall want some snow," he said. "Two or three bucketfuls at least."

Duncan went to the plain deal table, opened the bag. He saw the plan of his campaign plainly: combat the fever, sustain her flagging strength until the crisis.

First he made his patient comfortable, removing the huddle of twisted blankets, using one sheet to cover her. He had no ice. But Nature had given him an element as good and better. When the snow was brought in, he used it prodigally to pack the burning, emaciated frame.

Three packs he gave her, then read his thermometer by the oil lamp. The rising temperature was checked. He took the hypodermic and cautiously gave a minute dose of strychnine.

An hour passed. The two children had fallen asleep on the old horsehair sofa by the fire. The neighbor woman had ceased her suspicious lamentations and gazed at Duncan with a grudging interest and respect. McKelvie, too, seemed conscious of the effort being made.

"Doctor," he whispered, "do ye think she has a chance?"

"Be quiet, John McKelvie," the woman quickly intervened, "and let the doctor do his work."

Three o'clock in the morning came. Seated at the bedside, his hair disheveled, his collar open at the neck, his finger on his patient's wrist, Duncan felt a hollow sinking of his heart. For the past two hours he had been using strychnine freely; he had thrown all his forces into the struggle. The temperature was stationary, the breathing was no worse; but the pulse seemed at last to have passed beyond the limit of human aid. Under his fingers the beat fluttered, missed, fluttered feebly once again, and then went out.

"Ay," sadly murmured the woman at his side. "Ye've done your best, doctor, but she's gone."

CHAPTER 39

In his rebellion at the words, Duncan was swept by desperate inspiration. Swinging round, he took a vial of ether from the table, filled the syringe, and squeezed it into the left breast of the unconscious woman. Then, with both hands, using all his strength, he began to massage her flaccid heart. He worked frantically. For an instant there was no response; then beneath his hands he felt a slow, convulsive throb. The heart beat once, hesitated, ventured a second and a third, slowly resumed its uncertain rhythm.

Cramped though it was, he dared not change his position. He knew that every passing second was fighting on his side. Time, time—if only he could hold her till the crisis came.

She had not moved since the dreadful moment of her collapse. But now, suddenly, with a faint moan, she turned her head upon the pillow. A great, wild hope rose within him. Then he saw a single bead of sweat upon her brow. Spellbound, he watched it break, trickle slowly down her cheek. Another followed, and another. Soon she was bathed in perspiration, the fever had broken, the crisis was upon her—she was saved.

As Duncan finally rose wearily from the bedside, the first faint gleam of dawn was shining through the window. Utterly spent, he yet had a strange elation singing in his ears. Quietly he washed his face and hands in cold water, slowly drew on his jacket. And then, with a start, he became conscious of McKelvie.

The big forester stood watching him. "Doctor," he began, and then broke down. No litany of praise ever excelled that single, halting word, no thanks surpassed the sob that choked the woodsman's throat.

"Man, man! Don't be annoying the doctor," broke in the neighbor woman, bustling at the fire. "Here, doctor! Take this bowl of good pease brose. I've made some for the bairns' breakfast, and you shall have the first of it. There's no man more deserves it for this night's work."

Duncan sipped the hot, delicious brose with buttermilk. Never in all his life had he tasted anything so good. McKelvie ate with him, and Hamish, roused from the harness room, where he had spent the night, took his place beside them. The children, awakening, went to gaze with awe upon their sleeping mother, then joined the party at the table.

As Duncan drove back, the snow had ceased to fall and the sun was fingering the sky with red. Hamish for once was strangely talkative, the thaw of broken-down prejudice brought a flood of friendly gossip in its train. As they neared the village, he declared: "I know of one body who'll be pleased at what you've done. The doctor brought Annie McKelvie into the world. And sore grieved he was that she threatened to be taken!"

Duncan let himself into the house and slipped upstairs. Yet, though his tread was silent, Murdoch's voice called him as he passed across the landing. He paused, then went in.

"Well," said the old doctor in an odd tone, "did ye help the poor creature in her passing?"

Duncan made a tired, undramatic gesture. "She's going to get well. Had her crisis at four this morning. Damn your eyes, she'll be up before you will."

"Are ye jesting?" Murdoch asked.

"I am not," said Duncan wearily.

The old man's face was inscrutable. In a low voice he said: "Away and get two good hours' sleep. Ye've a hard day before ye. And the surgery's at nine."

There was nothing in the words to command attention. Yet the way Murdoch spoke them gave Duncan, as he went to his room, a glow of unspeakable content.

CHAPTER 40

Soon the whole community knew of Duncan's success with Annie McKelvie's pneumonia. There was no acclamation—merely a dry, terse recognition of the strange doctor's presence, coupled with the hope, piously expressed, that there might be good in the young man.

As the days went past, each brimming with incident, with strenuous medical and physical endeavor, Duncan felt an expansion of his ability. The pain of losing Margaret still lingered, and there were moments when a wave of desolation would sweep over him. Yet the wound was less severe than he could ever have believed.

The long gray days of snowfall had passed, and sometimes he covered fifty miles of rugged country in a morning's round, then came in, glowing and ravenous, for his midday meal. And always that meal was ready to be served, and savory, the moment he arrived. It amazed him that Jean should run the household with such quiet perfection.

One day, after he had been in Strath Linton two weeks, he said, "Jean, some man's going to get a good wife someday."

She turned away, so he could not see her face. In a restrained little voice she answered, "Do you think so?"

"I do indeed." His manner was half-joking. "And when your father retires, as he must do soon, and sets you up in style with a tidy dowry—"

She turned sharply, her expression agitated and intense. "Don't talk that way—it isn't like you!"

"Why, Jean—" He broke off, nonplussed.

"How can you be so smug about my future? Besides, you don't understand our position. Dad simply can't retire. He couldn't afford to. We're not rich, we're poor. We have nothing except this house and the furniture that's in it. My father hasn't run his practice to make a profit." A rush of pride swept into her distress. "All these years it's been a struggle to make ends meet. Even now we owe a big bill for drugs. And when you speak so stupidly about my marrying—" She stopped short, tears glistening in her eyes.

Though he could not guess the nature of his offense, he saw that he had hurt her. His voice was contrite. "I'm sorry, Jean. I was only trying to be funny."

"I'm stupid to get upset." She moved away, striving to control her voice. "Oh—I mustn't forget! A call came in just before lunch. Someone slightly injured at the hydroelectric plant at Loch Linton. Mr. Overton asked if you'd go up this afternoon."

"Overton," he echoed. "The hydroelectric plant!"

"Yes. If there's ever money made out of poor Strath Linton, he is the one that'll make it. With his cheap labor and bad materials."

In a strange, reflective mood, Duncan got into the car after lunch and drove off toward Loch Linton. The route mounted through the valley to the ridged plateau beyond. At length he reached the head of the glen, where the climax of assembled vistas should have burst upon him.

But there stretched no lovely mountain lake—only a new, man-made ugliness. Row after row of dismal shanties reached up from the shore. Trees had been ruthlessly slaughtered. All around were great, gashed-out mounds of earth. Dumps of refuse, tin cans, broken bottles cluttered the broken ground. At one side a chimney stack spouted smoke and sparks. At the other, big concrete mixers were laying the rough foundations of the aluminum works.

Leaving his car, he strode down a rough path to a hut marked: "Office, Keep Out." Three men were inside: Overton, a thickset man in overalls, and—to his surprise—Leggat, the lawyer from Levenford.

Honest Joe rose with a grunt of recognition. "You're here at last! I wondered when the devil you were coming. You know Mr. Leggat—my company's legal adviser. And Lem Briggs, my construction undermanager."

Duncan exchanged a nod with the unshaven Briggs, a

glance of bare recognition with the fox-faced solicitor. "I understand you've had an accident," he said.

"It's nothing," protested Honest Joe. "Only a bruised leg. Balk of timber gave way and some concrete fell on the fool below."

"The timber was sound," inserted Leggat. "It didn't break, it slipped." From his tone, Duncan knew the lawyer was lying. "Shall we take a look at him?" he said.

The injured workman lay in his bunk in one of the dormitories. With strongly aroused suspicions, Duncan made a close examination of the injury. Beneath the swelling, he made out a definite fracture.

"No bones broken, eh?" said Honest Joe, suggestively. "Not another compensation case. With every penny I've got sunk in this plant, I can't have that sort of nonsense."

"Transverse fracture of the fibula," said Duncan. "I'll report it tonight."

Honest Joe swore.

"That prop was rotten, Mr. Overton," said the workman. "I heard it crack. There's beetle in half the balks we're using."

"Shut up," Briggs said to him.

"Lem!" Leggat dripped oil. "You're too loyal to the company. They don't call Mr. Overton 'Honest Joe' for nothing. This poor feller'll get his wages all right. Even if he was entirely to blame we all know mistakes'll happen with the best men—" he paused—"and materials."

Honest Joe gave his lawyer a quick glance.

Duncan, meanwhile, was dressing the damaged leg, and now, with a few final touches, he adjusted it in a rudimentary cradle.

"Not a bad piece of work," commented Honest Joe, with unwilling admiration. "I'm downright glad ye worked your way up to be a doctor. Ye see a deal of my son, I understand?"

Duncan nodded.

"Eh, there's a lad to be proud of! With his prospects at the Wallace Foundation and this fine marriage he's making—he'll be top of the medical tree before you can say 'knife'!" He rubbed his hands together blandly. "Now, you'll never reach those heights, Stirling. But I wouldn't mind putting ye in the way of a nice post I have in mind—provided ye wouldn't want too much money. How are you gettin' on with old Murdoch down below?"

"Moderately." Duncan closed his bag with a noncommittal snap.

Honest Joe laughed unpleasantly. "You couldn't pull along with a slow old hack like him. Now, I've a notion my company could do with a doctor here, when we're organized and operating. You're the very man for the job. Keep it under your hat till I let you know further. Meantime, have a cigar?"

"Sorry, I must get back." Duncan parried the other's false friendliness. Then, at the pathway leading to his car, he paused and said coldly: "I'll just take the fee. That'll be half a guinea, please."

"What!"

"Unless—" Duncan gave him a level stare—"you think it should be more?"

Honest Joe mastered his chagrin after a moment, slowly took a ten-shilling note from his wallet, added a sixpence, and handed it to Duncan.

"There you are." He forced a smile. "I said you were an up-and-coming youngster. I don't dislike you for doin' a bit of business for yourself while the old man's on his back. As I said, you and me together one of these days. Better give me your address."

"I can be found in the medical register," Duncan said curtly.

"To be sure," said Overton, extending a damp hand. "I'll find you there—if I want you."

CHAPTER 41

On his way to the village, Duncan caught himself wiping his fingers as though to erase that clammy contact. The incident left a bad impression upon him, out of all proportion to its importance. The entire setup at the dam seemed spurious, untrustworthy. And behind Overton's half-offer he sensed some cunning motive. He had mind to tell Murdoch of the visit and his reaction. But in the end he decided not to worry the old man, for whom the mere mention of Overton envenomed the air. Instead, he slipped the half guinea in the tea caddy on the dresser, where Jean kept all the petty-cash takings of the practice. As he did so, he thought, "At least Honest Joe has paid for the Sunday dinner."

A month after Duncan's arrival in Strath Linton, Murdoch was able to get up and about. One afternoon, warmly wrapped in muffler, gloves, and ulster, he had just come in from pottering about the garden when Duncan returned from his round of visits.

Instantly there fell between them the singular constraint that marked their new relationship. Murdoch was well aware how hard the young doctor had worked the past four weeks, and secretly he knew he had misjudged him about Anna Geisler. Duncan, on his side, deeply regretted his past display of temper. Yet, though both longed for open reconciliation, neither wished to take the first step toward it.

"You've been in the garden," Duncan said quietly. "That's fine."

"Fine, my foot!" The old doctor scowled from sheer perversity. "Have ye killed a few more of my patients this afternoon? I'll need to call the roll when ye've gone, to find if there are any survivors left."

Duncan hung up his hat and coat on the mahogany stand. "You've stayed out too long. You need your tea. Where's Jean?" It was odd that she should not be on hand.

He called: "Jean! Your father wants his tea!"

"Be quiet, man," said Murdoch irritably. "Leave the lass alone. Retta'll fetch our tea for once."

Surprised, Duncan followed Murdoch into the sitting room, where a fire blazed. Presently the servant brought in the loaded tea tray.

"The room seems empty with just you and me," Duncan thought aloud.

"My daughter's dressing," Murdoch explained gruffly. "She's going to the Tenants' Ball tonight."

CHAPTER 42

Duncan repressed his surprise. He had known of the dance, of course—a feature in the winter social life of the district. But Jean had never mentioned her intention to attend it. Something of his surprise must have shown on his face, for Murdoch turned on him.

"What's the matter? Do ye grudge the lass one evening of pleasure, when she drudges her heart out every other day of the year?"

"No, no," said Duncan hastily. "It's just—well—I had no idea—" He stirred his tea much longer than was necessary. "Is she going alone?"

"She is not!" snapped Murdoch. "She's going with a young man who's paid her great attention for many a year."

Utterly taken aback, Duncan forced a smile. "And who might he be?"

Murdoch glanced queerly at Duncan. "Alex Aigle," he answered quietly. "A fine young fellow and Sir John Aigle's son."

Hiding his feelings, Duncan put down his cup, pulled out his briar, and slowly filled it. His recollection of the young man in the bus was highly flattering to Aigle. It had never occurred to him that Jean might have a suitor so desirable. He had taken her for granted, assumed her sweetness to be part of the Linton air. He could not analyze his dismay at the news.

It was then that Jean entered in her party dress. "Is there a cup of tea left?" she asked lightly.

He stared at her. He had never before seen her in anything but the plainest clothes. Her white chiffon frock was simple enough; yet, in its clinging freshness, emphasizing the lines of her youthful figure, it gave her new charm. Her hair, too, was done in a different style, with a white blossom tucked among its dark curls. Her eyes sparkled with anticipation of the dance.

Duncan said in a low voice: "Jean! You're as pretty—prettier than that flower in your hair."

Suddenly the front doorbell rang, and a moment later Aigle came in briskly, handsome in his black evening coat and white silk scarf.

"Good-evening, sir. Delighted to see you're better." He turned to Jean. "The first, fifth, ninth, and the last. And no refusals, please! If I don't book them now, I won't have a chance."

Jean blushed. "Such nonsense will go to my head. You've met Dr. Stirling, Alex?"

Aigle held out his hand. "I believe we shared a bus one night."

Duncan mumbled something inane. He was not good at small talk. The warmth of the welcome accorded to Aigle by Jean and her father added to his new dejection. Finally, still unhappily reticent, he saw Aigle help Jean into her cloak, saw them laughingly set off.

Later, in the surgery, he battled with a sense of loss and with anger, directed most of all against himself. And then, at nine o'clock, when he was halfway through, Retta came to the surgery door with a telegram.

He ripped open the envelope, quickly read: "Appointed for surgical research Wallace Foundation, Edinburgh. Commission also offers you pathology fellowship. Starting one week from now. Brilliant and exceptional opportunity. Strongly advise acceptance. Reply urgent. Geisler."

He thought with dark satisfaction: "I'm through with this petty country practice. Now I'm out only for myself. And by God, I'll show them all a thing or two before I'm through! Let her marry Aigle and be done with it."

He rapidly wrote the answer. "I will be there. We'll teach them something at the Wallace. Regards, Duncan."

CHAPTER 43

The post-mortem was over. Duncan, with a nod to his assistants, quitted the long, cold dissecting room in the basement of the Wallace Foundation. Mounting the private iron staircase, he entered his own quarters in the Department of Pathology.

As he stood recapitulating the lecture he would presently deliver, his expression was calculating, almost formidable. Harder, straighter, his face cast to a new authority by the two years he had spent in the Foundation, his brow had that puckered look which comes from close application to the microscope. His eyes were cold and ruthless.

His meditation was broken by a knock. It was Dr. Heddle, his junior assistant. "Dr. Geisler has phoned to ask when we can give her the medulla sections."

Duncan frowned. "This afternoon—at the latest. Tell her I'll look in on my way to the lecture theatre."

"Yes, sir." The junior paused, wondering if he dare say it. "By the way, Professor Lee was here, when you were in the dissecting room. He said these last neuroglial tissues are as good as anything he's seen in his fifty years' experience. I can't tell you how excited we all are that the big stunt's finishing so well."

Duncan nodded, not permitting himself to be moved by Heddle's loyalty or by the compliment from the principal of the Foundation. It was part of himself, the armed impassivity. The drive of his ambition was surer, now that it was cased in steel.

When the other had gone, he gathered up the sheaf of papers on his desk and went out through the busy laboratory, down a long corridor to the office of the surgical sub-chief, Dr. Geisler.

Anna was bent over the latest batch of microphotographs. Rather tensely, without looking up, she said, "Those chromosomes are showing definite partition."

"That's edifying."

"You might display a trifle more enthusiasm." With delicate fingers she swiveled the fine adjustment. "Considering they are on the verge of verifying your new theory."

He answered, unsmiling, "I knew that last night, when I examined the very slides you're looking at now."

Straightening, she brushed back her hair. "Here, after two years' grueling work, we are about to establish an epoch-making hypothesis of neuron regeneration—which will re-organize my technique on nerve surgery and send you up six flights on your medical career. And you—"

"D'you expect me to stand on my head?"

She threw up her hands. "The Scottish character is beyond me! Do everything—enjoy nothing!"

He viewed her with cynical detachment. "Enjoyment isn't in the program. When I set out to go through with this drudgery, I knew what I was doing—and where, exactly, I was going."

"Oh! I had a foolish idea you might be helping me."

"Don't worry. It doesn't matter who's driving our car; we're both going the same way," Duncan replied.

"Thanks for reassuring me. Which is your way?"

He shrugged his shoulders, and said: "In three years' time, I'll be the first medical consultant in Edinburgh. I shall roll out to see my cases—impress the local G.P.—rush my examination—prescribe on the way to the door. I shall never know—or care—whether my patients live or die. I shall be envied, admired, feared. In short—" his tone lost its mockery, became urgent—"I shall be famous!"

CHAPTER 44

Grudgingly she exclaimed: "Great heavens! Is this the starving yokel that once called Schumann's music a tune?" She frowned. "You've been too successful here. Our principal dotes on you. So do your assistants, and Chancellor Inglis, when he comes to town. You have double the number of students at your lectures that our dear Dr. Overton has, although he is your senior. By the way, are you going to his wife's reception tonight?"

He answered indifferently. "I suppose I'll look in."

"I shall, too," said Anna. "You know—I don't dislike her. She has improved quite a bit. It made me laugh at first, watching her establish her little salon, so gay and twittering, setting out to waft her handsome husband to the heights on her social triumphs. But now I don't laugh. I never laugh when I see a woman unhappy."

Duncan stared at her. "Unhappy? Nonsense!"

"Don't you think two years are long enough for the rosiest bride to discover she's married to a washout? Do you think it's pleasant to wake up every morning and look at his selfish, dissipated face and think, 'He isn't what I thought he was'?"

He said impatiently, "What drivel you talk!"

"Do I?" She smiled mockingly. "But we both know Dr. Overton, do we not?"

"He's harmless."

"Is he? My dear Duncan, watch out for that man! His jealousy of you amounts to a disease. And he has powerful friends."

"I've taken care of myself in the past."

"But in the future, the immediate future—" She broke off significantly.

Hands deep in his jacket pockets, he tried to probe her meaning. Then, abruptly, he dismissed it. "I have a lecture in

105

precisely half a minute. I can't stand here crystal gazing. We'll discuss the final revisions of the proofs tonight."

When the lecture was over, he went to his clinic in the outer wing of the department. In front of his desk stretched a long line of men and women from the humbler walks of life, sent by their doctors from all over the country for some special pathological test. The institution's great reputation made it the magnet for such cases. Yet nowadays they were less patients to Duncan than units in an inhuman chain, which he turned expertly, working the treadmill of his ambition.

Today he was more than usually brusque—briefly scanning the admission cards, throwing out particulars to his secretary, setting his assistants to work at diagnostic tests.

Suddenly a wave of uneasiness swept over him. He paused, involuntarily raised his head. At first he could not believe his eyes. Halfway down the line of patients, awaiting her turn with the others, was his mother.

CHAPTER 45

He disposed of the intervening cases as though in a dream. Then she stood before him, his own mother, no trace of recognition in her calm, drawn face, offering him the letter of introduction from her doctor.

As he accepted it, his composure nearly broke. All around were his students, a roomful of patients, his secretary, copying the particulars from the admission card. Martha Stirling. Age, fifty-nine. Abruptly he opened the letter.

When he had read it, he dared not look at her. In a voice scarcely recognizable, he said: "Please go into dressing-room A. I will attend to you myself."

Five minutes later, he confronted her in the small, screened cubicle. "Mother!"

She was sitting on the deal chair, a pathetic figure, a hospital blanket around her bare shoulders. But the old unyielding grimness was in her eyes.

"Dr. Logan of Levenford sent me here. I wouldn't have come if I'd known it was you." The same stubbornness that had made her refuse his advances, his presents of money, his offers of support, still possessed her.

He said hurriedly: "You'll let me see what's troubling you, Mother? Dr. Logan seems uncertain."

"He's afraid that I have cancer." Now, as always, she did not mince her language.

As she slowly pulled off the blanket, his heart contracted at the sight of a small, deep ulcer. Sick with apprehension, he asked, "When did this come?"

"I stumbled against the dresser six weeks ago. I didn't heed it at the time. But afterward—"

He stared fixedly at the lesion, with growing fear that it was malignant. "I must examine a few cells under the microscope. That'll tell us whether it's something bad or nothing at all. Do you understand?"

She nodded valiantly.

He picked up a vial of ethyl chloride. He had to fight to keep his voice from breaking. "This spray is a local anesthetic. I won't hurt you."

"Maybe ye think ye have hurt me enough already."

She watched him remotely, her features pinched, worn, yet tranquil as a few moments later he stained the specimen, then slipped it beneath the microscope.

His fingers trembled as he turned the fine adjustment; his vision was blurred. At last he made out a cluster of normal cells. His heart thudded with suspense. Still he searched, without sign of the dreadful cancer forms, until, with grateful certainty, he picked out a group of staphylococcal bacteria. The ulcer was not malignant, but a simple infection, which could unquestionably be cured.

CHAPTER 46

He was so unnerved, he dared not turn around. For a moment he remained bowed over the microscope, collecting his emotions. Finally he said: "It isn't serious after all! There's no growth of any kind."

Her expression barely changed. But she took a quick breath. "Are you speaking the truth?"

"In a month you'll be perfectly well."

It seemed for a moment as though she weakened. Then, straightening her thin body, she was herself again. "It's the Lord's will, whatever happens to us. I'm grateful to Him for sparing me this added cross."

With longing for self-justification, he ignored the implication. "Mother! Your coming here like this seems more than accidental, almost as though Providence wanted to prove to both of us—" He broke off. "Doesn't it mean anything that I've been able to do this for you today?"

"Couldn't someone else have done it?"

He flinched. "Will you never give me credit? Here am I, by my own efforts, in the most famous medical institute in the country, making my way to the top—and yet, when we're thrown together, when I can take away from you a sentence of death, you still hold your bitter prejudice against me."

She studied him without expression. "I'm not impressed by what ye tell me and still less by what I see. Ye don't look well—nor happy, either. Ye're white and drawn. There's lines on your brow and a touch of gray about your temples. Ye've a hard, dissatisfied air, as though ye sought for something and couldn't find it."

"But I will find it," he said hotly. "I'm on my way to the top. And when I'm there, I'll reach out my hands and take everything I want."

"What does it matter?" She drew her old coat about her

shoulders. "Thirty shillings a week or thirty thousand a year? Whether ye wear fine broadcloth or homespun tweed? The test comes when folks follow you with their eyes, as ye walk down the street, and say to themselves, 'There goes a fine, a worthy man!' "

He was about to answer when the screen of the cubicle was pulled aside and Dr. Heddle appeared with a group of students behind him.

"There's a case waiting, which you must see. We think it needs full serological investigation. Can any of us help you finish here?"

Duncan shook his head. With his students crowding in upon him, it was impossible to prolong the interview. "I must leave you now. You have no cause for anxiety whatsoever," he reassured his mother.

Taking a pad, he wrote rapidly: "Come and see me six o'clock tonight at my rooms, No. 24, Princes Crescent. You still misjudge me. I want your affection and esteem. I want to provide for your future." He signed it—from habit or from grim perversity—"Duncan Stirling, M.D."

That night, though Duncan waited long and eagerly for her, she did not arrive. He had known in his heart that she would not come; but the blow was cruel nonetheless. A bitter desire for escape, more than anything else, made him think of Margaret's party.

CHAPTER 47

It was after nine-thirty when he climbed the steps of the Overton home in one of Edinburgh's best districts. Up-stairs, the cream-colored drawing room was full. As he entered, Margaret came quickly forward to greet him.

"Duncan!" she exclaimed. "I'm so glad. I was afraid you weren't coming."

He tried to be gay. "You'd never have missed me, in a pack like this."

"But I would!" she protested quickly.

She had, he thought, a keyed-up air. Her eyes were very bright, and there were faint shadows beneath them. She had a new, restless, provoking quality, which might have stirred the pulse of any man.

"You know everyone here," she said.

He glanced indifferently around the room, recognizing about thirty people. Dr. Overton, glass in hand, with a group around him; Mrs. Inglis; Professor Lee of the Foundation; Colonel Scott; young Dr. Heddle; Anna; several of the doctors from the Wallace; and a sprinkling of advocates from the Parliament House.

"Don't bother about me, Margaret. I'll find my way around."

At that moment two other guests arrived. As she left his side, she murmured, "We'll have a chance to talk later."

He stood a moment, picked up a whisky and soda from the tray offered him. Although he detested these dull, pre-tentious parties, he forced himself to attend them. They were part of his new existence, a means to an end, rungs on the ladder of his ambition.

Colonel Scott, standing with Mrs. Inglis, gave him a friendly nod as he approached. The Colonel, grayer, sparer with the passing years, had a look of strain about him. Apparently his rumored involvement in the Linton Hydroelectric scheme, now at last nearing completion, had taken heavy toll of his finances and his energy. Perhaps the knowledge that his worries were drawing to an end threw an added joviality into his greeting.

"'Evening, Stirling. You look well!"

"Have you heard the news?" Mrs. Inglis asked. "Professor Lee has just announced his retirement."

For a moment Duncan did not grasp it. Then his boredom vanished. "Is that official?"

"Quite. In three months the Foundation will have a new principal. As the wife of the chancellor, it might be indiscreet of me to prophesy who it will be."

He knew instantly whom she meant. Her partiality for Overton was notorious! Since his marriage to her niece, he had openly become her protégé. She smiled triumphantly at Duncan's chagrin.

"I thought you'd enjoy that information."

She led the Colonel away. From across the room Duncan saw Anna watching him. Was this the reason for her warning earlier? He had to know more, quickly. He went over to the group surrounding Dr. Overton.

Overton looked excited and mildly drunk. His flushed and rather flabby face showed how much he had run to seed in the past two years.

"Hello, Stirling. Heard the burning topic?"

"I've heard."

"It's a wonderful post for somebody," Heddle sighed.

"There'll be plenty of competition," said another.

"The competition should be limited," Overton broke in authoritatively. "In the first place, a young man ought to get it."

"Someone about your age," suggested Anna, over Duncan's shoulder.

There was a laugh. Overton gulped his whisky defiantly.

"Why not? I've as much right to the chair as anybody. The Commission wants someone with push and go. It's only fair a doctor from the Foundation should have the preference. I'm the senior lecturer. And I have first-class qualifications."

A short silence followed this declaration. Then in an odd, reflective tone, Anna remarked, "As a matter of fact now you put it that way—you do seem to have a pretty good chance, Overton."

"Well—maybe." Overton made a show of caution. He turned to Duncan with a smile. "What do you think, Stirling?"

"I'm your guest here tonight. I'd rather not say."

Overton colored. "Afraid to give your opinion?"

Duncan could stand it no longer. He said recklessly: "I don't think you're quite the man for the job, Overton. The chair should go to a first-class physician."

"And so it will," said Overton. "I'll back my chance against the best they can produce."

"If that is a bet," Duncan countered, "I'm prepared to take it."

CHAPTER 48

Overton's guests stared at him oddly. He realized that he might wreck his almost certain chances by a clumsy scene. With an inaudible remark he turned away hurriedly to replenish his glass.

The little group about Duncan scattered. He felt utterly depressed. Suddenly he felt a touch upon his sleeve. Turning, he found Margaret beside him.

"I've been wondering when you'd recognize my existence." She smiled. "Come and have a drink."

He let her lead him into the deserted buffet, where she poured two glasses of champagne.

"Dear Duncan! You looked so glum, and you could be quite amusing if you tried."

"I will be if I drink that champagne. Honestly, Margaret, I mustn't mix my drinks."

But she would take no refusal. "Let's drink a toast to the future—and to ourselves!" There was a touch of recklessness in her tone, as, after touching the rim of his goblet with hers, she emptied her own.

"I drink to the past, too, Margaret—the future may be quite a mess."

She shook her head. "No, no, Duncan. There are good things to come—for us!" She opened the French window that led to a small balcony. "Let's begin by taking a look at the moon. It's nearly full, and quite lovely."

He followed her, his uneasiness increasing as she closed the curtained window, screening them upon this tiny balcony high over the silent city. The moon was truly superb—a great white disk shining behind the castle battlements, above the deep shadows of the gardens adjoining Princes Street.

She sighed. "We never looked at a moon together in the old days, did we, Duncan?"

"No," he answered drily.

"If we had, it might have made—quite a difference."

"I wonder, Margaret."

"Oh, Duncan, I made a sad mistake."

"I'm sorry, Margaret," he answered uncomfortably, looking away from her, staring into the night. "Perhaps it'll all straighten out after a bit. Marriage can be difficult at first; but when two people learn to make allowances, they often grow closer to one another."

"Don't serve up that platitude. I've had enough of it from my aunt. Why not let me say it outright? I've made a ghastly blunder." She put her hand on his sleeve, with bright, engaging frankness. "You were the real one for me. There! That's the truth. I found it out only when it was too late."

CHAPTER 49

Quickly, with a touch of compunction, she went on. "My husband's not a bad fellow. He can be charming when he chooses. That's why I married him, I suppose. But he's so self-centered, so superficial. He's a brag and a bore. When he's had too much to drink, he's beastly. Besides, he can't leave women alone—other women, I mean. I've caught him in two affairs. And there was something really serious—I've never quite found out—with a nurse, before we were married." She paused. "I needed someone with depth, with real strength and resources." She added in a low voice, "In fact, I still need someone like that."

"Didn't you mention that it was too late, Margaret?"

"But is it? Is it, Duncan? Oh, I don't mean the obvious thing. I'll keep up the outward show for my father's sake. But between you and me, Duncan, life's so short, it seems such a pity to waste it." He compelled himself to look at her. She was leaning back against the coping, her figure outlined by her soft gown. The moonlight gave her upturned face a provocative beauty. There was no mistaking the invitation in her eyes.

All his old desire for her came flowing back. At last he saw her as she was—a bored and spoiled woman—and he realized now what her only appeal for him had been. Yet his mood of perverse recklessness made him reach out and take her in his arms. She bent back her head, kissed him with a lingering, expert mouth.

Suddenly, inexplicably, her lips made him hate himself. He put her away from him with rough abruptness.

"You don't know what we're doing, Margaret."

"No one need ever know," she answered quickly.

"Margaret, I've no time for that sort of thing. Women can't exist for me any more. They don't belong in my life."

She smiled, provoked by his resistance, yet sure of her

power over him. "There must be room for me! Oh, Duncan, I feel that my own life's beginning all over again."

"I couldn't, Margaret—because I once loved you."

Her voice rose incredulously. "You mean you don't love me any more?"

He remained motionless, his head bent. "I'm sorry, Margaret."

Her pride had never been so affronted. Her features were drawn and sharpened, her voice was edged with sudden spite. "Let's go in. I'm cold."

CHAPTER 50

He left the party immediately. To his acute annoyance, he found Anna on the front porch ready to leave.

"Shall I drop you on my way?" she asked.

Still overcome by conflicting emotions, he said, "I'm walking home."

"Then I'll walk, too."

"Anna, for once I prefer my own to your company."

"So! Then you shall have my company."

Her persistence infuriated him. But she was not to be put off. Though he walked rapidly, she kept up with him. And soon, with amiable irony, she remarked, "Quite a pleasant evening, my friend, for a charming balcony scene."

He ignored her.

Unperturbed, she went on. "But it would appear that Romeo didn't quite come up to scratch. Fool!"

He still did not answer.

"I have always thought," she reflected, "that a man in such circumstances should—shall I say—dine, at the risk of a momentary moral indigestion, if he is hungry."

It was too much. The day, with all its disillusionment, the evening, with its bitter implications, had left him with an angry sense of futility and distrust. "For heaven's sake, shut up!" he said viciously to Anna.

"My dear doctor! I was merely being metaphysical, or if you prefer it, biological. I've been watching you these last few months. All this sublimation is going to land you in trouble—besides keeping you off your work. Why don't you go out and get drunk, or make a fool of yourself for once? Now, especially, I want you to be an amenable human being—not a stick of repressed dynamite about to go off at any minute."

"What the devil do you mean—now, especially?"

"Just this: I want you to apply for the principalship of the

Foundation."

He laughed harshly. "That already belongs to Dr. Overton."

"It will if you don't apply. Listen, Duncan," she hurried on persuasively, "you're young, untried; but you're the only man in the Foundation with genuine ability. Professor Lee knows that. Besides, you wouldn't want Overton to get the chair—he'd ruin the Foundation."

"Why don't you apply yourself?"

"They'd never give it to a woman." She kept her resentment from her voice. "That's why I depend on you."

"What do you expect to get out of this?" he asked cynically.

"All the pull that friendship with the principal will give me. A new operating room, a couple of research assistants, and an extra ward, dedicated to my new neuromuscular technique."

"Not much!"

She countered swiftly. "Do you grudge me a small fee—for my professional services to you?"

"Must you throw that at me again?" After a pause, he said sharply: "I haven't got the faintest chance. But, as it happens, I've already made up my mind to go for this thing. I want it for every reason in the world. It's my big chance at last—to fight Overton and his vested interests. I've owed him something for ten long supercilious years. Now I'm going to render my account." His words suddenly took on an overwhelming fierceness. "What is the whole thing, anyway, but a rotten skin game? Success! That means kicking the next man down and trampling on him. And life! It's just a dirty game of beggar-my-neighbor. All right! I can play that game as well as anyone can."

"And why shouldn't you?" she exclaimed elatedly. "Now you see what this means? You'll be a specialist long before you expected it."

They had reached the entrance to the house where he had his rooms, a high, narrow dwelling in one of the terraces close to Princes Street. He brought out his latchkey.

"Your faith in me is most touching, Anna. One word more, and I'll burst into tears. Good-night."

As he turned the key in the lock, she said eagerly: "You'll send in your application this week? The earlier it's in, the better."

"Damn you!" he answered roughly. "Haven't I told you I'm going into it right up to the neck?" His voice rose suddenly to breaking point. "Now get out of here before I slam this door in your scheming face!"

"But, Duncan—" Impulsively she reached out her hand, her cynicism gone, her whole expression melting to swift regret.

He could not see, in the darkness, the new spark of tenderness in her eyes. He wished only to get away. Before she could speak again, he went into the house and closed the door quietly.

CHAPTER 51

The following Friday Duncan left the Foundation after a momentous day. That morning he had sent in his application for the principalship, and his face showed a keen purposefulness as he swung out of Princes Street toward his rooms. Suddenly he stopped. Advancing down the street toward him was a rough-clad country figure.

"Hamish!"

"Ay, none other, doctor!" The man from Strath Linton clasped Duncan's outstretched hand.

Red of face and thatch, ill at ease in his black Sunday clothes with celluloid dickey and greased, heavy boots, he remarked shyly: "It's long enough since I clapped eyes on ye, doctor. As I happened to be in Edinburgh, I thought I might give ye a call. Though ye're such a figure now, ye wouldn'a have time for the likes of me!"

"Nonsense, Hamish, man! I'm delighted to see you! Come into my rooms and take some refreshment."

When Hamish was safe inside, seated on the edge of a chair with his cap on his knee, a glass of neat whisky in one hand and a hunk of Scots shortbread in the other, he saluted, "Here's health, doctor!"

"The best to you, Hamish!" Duncan responded. "But come along now, what's the news? What are you doing in Edinburgh?"

"Well, I had a few jobs to do. Shoppin', buyin' a few drugs, and the like."

Duncan was puzzled. "I thought you bought your drugs in St. Andrews."

"Ay, we did, we did," Hamish agreed unthinkingly. "But now we go to a new company. They're cheaper."

"Oh!" Duncan suddenly drew up.

"Besides—" embarrassed, feeling the need of further explanation, the big man blundered on—"I had more to do than buy drugs. I had some of Dr. Murdoch's old books to sell!"

"What!" Duncan stared at his visitor. Taking his pipe from the mantelpiece, he began to fill it. "I suppose all's well at Strath Linton?"

"Ay, ay," said Hamish hastily. "We keep going. Of course, the master has failed a trifle lately. It's hard going for a man of seventy."

"He should have an assistant."

"Assistant!" echoed Hamish with a twist of his mouth. "He had four in six months!"

"How so?" asked Duncan quickly.

Hamish gave a sheepish smile. "They fumbled and bungled, wouldn't gang out on night calls, stripped the gears of the car, gave the wrong medicines. Oh, they drove the master fair demented, till he took and threw every one of them out of the house." A pause. "We've had nobody right, since we had yourself, doctor."

Duncan struck a match fiercely. "Surely somebody would have suited. I know lots of capable young fellows. I'll pick one out and send him down."

The whisky had loosened Hamish's tongue. "It's no use, Dr. Stirling. The practice cannot be run by an assistant now."

"In God's name!" Duncan swung round and began to pace up and down. "Why not?"

"Ye see," Hamish took a long breath. "We've got opposition now! A rival doctor, brought in by Overton. His name's Bailey. He takes orders from the mealymouthed contractor. In return, he has all the twelve hundred workmen at the Aluminum and Hydroelectric Plant. They're forced to have him—like it or not. He's the Company's man! Ye ken how the auld doctor never charged fees. It was the Insurance Cards brought in the money. And now he hasn't got more than a dozen cards! I'm telling ye, it's nip-and-tuck to keep things going!"

Shocked, Duncan stopped short, seeing the entire picture.

"Ooh, we'll win through," said Hamish with a show of

cheerfulness. "In any case, I'm proper glad to have seen ye, doctor. Miss Jean bade me tell ye that ye're always welcome, if ye're ever near to Linton."

At the mention of Jean's name, Duncan's figure drew more rigidly together. He saw her struggling against hardship, facing adversity with bright and tranquil courage. He realized he had never stopped loving her, and even as he did, he remembered something else.

"I suppose she sees quite a lot of young Aigle still."

"Ay, ay!" Hamish nodded emphatically. "Alex is always about the house. He thinks the world of her. He's been in Canada these last two months. But we expect him back the end of the year."

"I daresay things will look up for Murdoch then. And for Jean?"

"To be sure they will," Hamish smiled confidentially. "Alex wants to marry her, ye ken!"

CHAPTER 52

After Hamish left, Duncan contemplated the simple gifts which the McKelvies had sent by him. He recalled the forester's modest home as it was that snowy night, the woman sick to death—the woman he had healed.

That had been real and wonderful. "God," he reflected, "have I done anything at all since then?"

But what did it matter now—that drama of the snows? And why should the petty misfortunes of an aging country doctor concern him? He had stamped all emotion from his life. His future career depended on that. Anyway, a rich, successful marriage would take care of the Murdochs' troubles!

Three days after Hamish's visit, Duncan saw Dr. Overton for the first time since the reception.

Toward half-past twelve that Monday, he strode into Overton's office with a sheaf of reports. "Here are the results on three of your cases, Overton," he announced formally.

Glancing up sharply from his desk, Overton hesitated, then changed his manner to a pleasant negligence. "Thanks! Decent of you to fetch them along. By the way, Stirling! I heard a wild sort of rumor that you were applying for the Chair. Is it true?"

"Quite true," Duncan answered curtly.

"You know," Overton said, "it seems a pity that you and I should be in active competition once again." He shrugged his shoulders pleasantly. "In the end, one of us has got to go under."

"I appreciate your consideration!"

"As a matter of fact," Overton reflected with a show of logic, "I am considering you, Stirling. Why can't you stay put in a post which is bringing you forward so nicely?"

"Not shake up the apple cart?"

"Exactly. It seems to me that your prospects here, in your particular field, are wonderful. Now if you thought it over, and made up your mind to continue in your own department and not interfere—"

"You'd give me every conceivable facility and the keys of the Kingdom of Heaven when they've made you Principal!" Duncan finished derisively.

Overton flushed. "I'm only trying to spare you an inevitable humiliation."

"I'll put up with that!"

"You'll put up with a darned sight more!" Overton choked with temper. "When I do get the Chair, I'll see you get what you deserve! You'll laugh out of the other side of your face when you take marching orders from me!"

"I've never taken an order from you, and I don't think I ever will!"

"We'll see!" Overton shouted, his caution gone. "Here's one to begin with! Don't try to make love to Margaret. She happens to be my wife—not yours!"

CHAPTER 53

"What exactly do you mean?" Duncan demanded.

"What I say. You've been making a play for her for months!"

"If only for your wife's sake, you'll take that back, Overton!"

"I'll be damned if I will!" Overton blustered. "We all know your reputation with women! At St. Andrews you had everybody talking about your affair with Anna! D'you think I'm fool enough to let that happen with my wife?"

Duncan took a step toward the other man. "Say you're lying, Overton, or I'll beat the life out of you!"

"I'm not lying! Margaret told me herself!"

At that moment Margaret walked into the room. She stood there, composed and elegant, perfectly conscious of the scene she had interrupted, ignoring Duncan, smiling brightly toward her husband.

"Coming to lunch, dear?"

Overton tugged out his handkerchief, mopped his brow. "Yes, Margaret, I'm coming, if our amorous friend has no objection!"

For the first time she showed her awareness of Duncan's presence, and nodded distantly.

Then she observed, "Really, my good Don Juan, you should pay some attention to your wardrobe."

"You think so, Margaret?"

"I do, indeed!" She laughed brightly. "I couldn't help remarking your rustic style the other night at our house."

"Perhaps I'd better not come again."

"Well, I don't suppose we shall see much of you this winter. I've planned to do a lot of entertaining in support of Euen's candidacy. And, under the circumstances, you'd hardly wish to be there."

"Quite right," he agreed.

She adjusted her smart hat. "I've been so busy since this vacancy for the principalship came along! Everyone thinks Euen'll get it. He's so popular. I feel sure he will. I'm going to help him all I can."

Placing her hand lightly on Overton's arm, she swept out of the room. Duncan had no chance to speak. It was clear she had misrepresented to her husband the incident on the balcony. He knew that now she would work with Overton, using every means to discredit him with the Commission and Professor Lee.

Outside the office, he ran unexpectedly into a burly figure in a bowler hat and raincoat. It was Honest Joe himself.

"Hello, hello!" cried the contractor jovially. He had been hurrying and was slightly short of breath. "The very man I'm looking for! I'm takin' my boy and his wife out to lunch. Care to come along?" He was too ingratiating.

"Not today, thanks."

"Well, I'm downright sorry. Can I have a word with ye? It won't take but a minute! Look here now, doctor! We've had our misunderstandings. But I've always been your friend. Remember that talk we had at the dam? That's what I'm here about. I meant to come months ago. I've been so rushed I never had a second. But now I've come personally to offer you the position—" he brought it out with an air— "of physician and surgeon to the Eastern Counties Power Company."

"I understood you had a doctor," Duncan drawled.

"Oh, we have! Dr. Bailey! But not in your class at all. Now that the Company's opening up, I want a topnotch medico. And I'm prepared to pay for him! A thousand a year, all the insurance takings, and a nice little packet of preferred stock in the Company besides."

This new approach was so obvious it was insulting. Honest Joe was afraid that he might interfere with his son's career. Angered beyond words, Duncan turned abruptly and entered his own department, leaving Honest Joe marooned and speechless in the corridor.

CHAPTER 54

By the end of November, three candidates had been singled out by public opinion as having the likeliest chances of success. In order of preference, they were: Dr. Overton; Chivers, an English Professor from Durham University; and Duncan.

The hot discussion throughout the Foundation and the local medical fraternity as to who would ultimately be chosen overflowed into the city press, where the forthcoming election was headlined as a major event. Photographs of Overton began to appear, accompanied by pictures of his wife, with such assertive captions as: "Principal Designate of the Wallace Foundation" and "Dr. and Mrs. Overton to be honored by the Foundation." Honest Joe's money was at work.

Shortly after that, the campaign took a more vicious turn. In a widely read gossip column of the *Evening Tribute*, a suggestive paragraph appeared. It was headed: "Doctor Lothario!" While skirting libel, it reopened the gossip which had coupled Duncan's name with Anna's at St. Andrews.

Duncan fumed, but made himself ignore it. When the slander was repeated the following Monday in the *Morning Argus*, in an even more scandalous form, he took the newspaper to Anna.

"I've got to do something!" He paced up and down while she read it. "Contradict it! Smash up the editor's office! Give Overton the whipping of his life!"

"My dear Duncan, do you remember a certain charming bunch of letters? In case you don't, I'll refresh your memory."

She unlocked her bureau, and gave him a blue-ribboned packet of letters. They were the ones Overton had written to Nurse Dawson.

"No, Anna! We couldn't use these. It's a vile trick. I refused before—"

"There was no need before! Are you going to let them smear you all over the town and not hit back? I tell you Heaven has delivered them into our hands. We'll sit still, let them poison the Commission with this muck, and then—at the last minute—fling this bombshell right into the tea party!"

"My God!" he said. "What a killing!"

"I could even get Nurse Dawson to appear. I've kept track of her. She's in the Glasgow General now! She has no tender feelings for dear Dr. Overton."

Slowly he gripped her hand. "It's on, Anna! I told you I was in this to my neck! I can push through muck with the rest of them."

From that day, he attacked on every front to assure his chances. He intensified the work of his department, working himself early and late. In December he published with marked success his second monograph on "Regeneration of the Neuron" in the *Journal of Medicine*.

Still he refused to rest upon his laurels. Hating the dry technicality of these researches, he nevertheless outlined at fever heat a fresh investigation: "The Pathology of Muscular Incoordination." And having issued the précis in *The Annals of Science*, flung himself into it vigorously.

CHAPTER 55

One rainy December afternoon, when darkness had fallen and the light and warmth of the department were enclosed by drawn blinds, Duncan looked up from his test bench to find Professor Lee watching him.

"I'm sorry, sir," he apologized. "I didn't hear you."

"Don't apologize! I've only come to invite you to dinner."

"To dinner!" Duncan echoed, astonished.

"At my house, tonight, eight o'clock sharp." The quiet old man's eyes twinkled. "I understand you haven't been about to many parties lately. At least, I haven't seen you at Mrs. Overton's house!"

"No, sir." Duncan looked down.

"Strange, for one who is such a ladies' man, eh, Stirling?" Lee beamed. "They give you quite a reputation in the local press."

Duncan's face flushed.

"Well!" The Professor rubbed his hands together softly. "Tonight at my house, there'll be no women—only men. I want you to meet the members of the Foundation Committee. Dr. Inglis you already know, and Judge Lenzie, Professor Brandt, Dr. Gibson, and I will be there."

It was impossible to misunderstand the significance behind the invitation or its friendliness.

"It's very kind of you, sir! Of course I'm delighted! I'll be there!"

"Good!" The other man nodded. "I warn you there will be a burning curiosity to hear your answer to certain recent allegations. Have a good lie ready!"

"I'll prefer to tell the truth, sir."

Lee chuckled. "By the way, I read your second monograph last night. It might have been worse."

After he had gone, Duncan stood at his bench, his

thoughts racing jubilantly. He barely heard the door reopen, as Anna came in, dressed in hat and raincoat. "Have you forgotten we're going to the opera tonight?"

"You'll have to go alone, Anna," he said calmly. "I'm busy."

Half-frowning, she perched on the edge of the bench. "Duncan," she said with a peculiar compunction, that strange note of regard which had lately crept into her attitude toward him, "I know your grim tenacity, your Scots determination. But, my friend, when I urged you on to this, I didn't mean you to kill yourself. You're no use to me dead!"

"Don't worry, I'm very much alive!"

"You're getting hollow in the cheeks and—yes, more than a little dusty around the temples. You don't have any exercise. Even if you won't come to the opera, you should have some sport—golf, tennis—" Her voice trailed off, diffident, oddly maternal.

He looked at her from beneath his brows, wondering what had come over her. "Golf! Tennis! Heavens! No, Anna, I've got more important things on my mind." He scanned her sideways. "Dining with Professor Lee, for instance!"

"What!" She sat up.

"I had the Principal in here five minutes ago." He paused. "He was rather decent—joked about our friend's publicity campaign. And then invited me to eat with the Committee!"

He had never seen her so stirred before. Her voice shook. "But don't you see what it means?" She was almost incoherent. "The whole thing's plain as daylight! Lee wants you to succeed him. I've always known he was fond of you. If you play your cards properly—" Her voice rose. "They're sure to pump you on the smear campaign. Work up their curiosity to the limit. When the wine goes around after dinner, make a great show of reluctance. Then bring out the Dawson letters!"

He nodded grimly. "It's the God-given moment."

"Grüss Gott!" she exulted. "If I could only see their faces.

131

It'll be a riot! You're as good as in the Chair!"

"Oh, be quiet, Anna!" he said sharply. "I'm not there yet."

But he could not silence her. She talked on excitedly, congratulating him, marching up and down the lab. At last, however, he was rid of her, and went back to his work.

CHAPTER 56

When Duncan reached home, there was half an hour to spare before he need dress and go out again into the incessant rain. He relaxed in an easy-chair with a drink before a snug fire and picked up the evening paper. He turned the sheets indifferently until he came unexpectedly upon an item of late news.

"Disaster at Strath Linton.

"This afternoon the floods due to the recent heavy rains produced an unfortunate accident at the newly completed dam of the Eastern Counties Hydroelectric Power Plant. Pressure of the swollen loch killing five and injuring seven. In the work of extrication, which went on for over an hour, Dr. Murdoch, who had been called to the scene to assist Dr. Bailey, the company doctor, was struck and crushed by a block of falling masonry. His injuries are believed to be serious."

Appalled, Duncan read the paragraph twice. His thoughts flashed back to that first night when the country doctor had befriended him, then swift across the ten succeeding years of friendship—and coolness. Murdoch, crushed by a block of falling masonry, serious injuries. . . .

Duncan jumped up. He forgot his engagement with Lee. Everything but the thought of Murdoch's accident was erased from his mind. He glanced at the clock. His car was in a nearby garage. With luck he could be in Linton by nine.

The rain had deepened to a downpour, and as he raced across the sodden countryside the water flew from the body of the car in two high trajectory waves. Everywhere, by the blurred glare of his headlights, he saw the evidence of the prolonged rainfall in flooded fields, running ditches, rivers roaring high beneath their bridges.

The speed of his reckless passage seemed to ease his tension. He was nearing his objective. All at once, out of the swimming darkness, his beam picked up a yellow barrier across the road with a man beside it, frantically flagging him. Only by a miracle did he draw up in time.

The patrolman splashed up to the window of the car in his dripping yellow oilskins. "What way's that to drive on a night like this? Turn right around. Ye can go no farther!"

"Why?" Duncan threw the query into the glare made by the road scout's torch.

"The Strath Linton road's flooded. The dam's liable to burst any minute."

Duncan made no protest, but while the other talked, he silently slipped the car in gear. The car shot forward, splintering the wooden barrier, smashing the obstructing planks aside.

The route, though more heavily flooded, was not impassable. On an impulse, Duncan switched on the dashboard radio. Immediately he heard the news that he was seeking.

"The threat to Strath Linton," said the dispassionate voice of the announcer, "is more serious than was at first anticipated. There is no sign of cessation of the rain, and the crack in the new Hydroelectric Alumina Dam on Loch Linton appears to be widening. Relief workers are already on the spot. While the situation remains well in hand, according to a statement issued by Mr. Joseph Overton and other officials of the Company, all traffic has been diverted from the area, and as a precautionary measure the inhabitants of the glen have been advised temporarily to leave their homes." The voice took on a graver tone. "A bulletin has just come in announcing that the death toll is now fifteen. Dr. Murdoch of Strath Linton, who was caught beneath the falling masonry while rescuing an injured man, is more critically hurt than was originally announced. It is feared that the doctor may not recover."

CHAPTER 57

Duncan crushed the accelerator to the floorboards. The car roared on. Ten miles ahead he swung into a familiar side road, passing two farm wagons loaded with household goods. Another five miles, and he was in the village of Linton. He stopped the car opposite the doctor's house and jumped out. The rain hit him in a solid wall. The street was deserted.

Retta, in coat and hat, let him in.

"Retta! Where's Dr. Murdoch?"

She raised a quivering, tear-stained face. "They've kept him up at the plant, Dr. Stirling."

"Then where's Miss Jean?"

"She's up there, too." The maid broke down. "Everybody's gone. And I'm goin', too."

She hurried off down the street.

Outside again in that drenching night, Duncan could see no one, until a spare and solitary figure abruptly rounded the corner. Duncan shouted with relief as he recognized the straggler.

"McKelvie!"

"Dr. Stirling!"

"Heavens! I'm glad to see you, man!" Duncan caught his arm. "I've got to get up to the plant!"

"It's not possible," McKelvie answered with decision. "The road's carried away."

"But I must. Don't ye see, man, Murdoch's up there. I must get to him, I must!"

McKelvie stroked his lean, wet jaw. "Well," he said at last. "Ye cannot make it by the road. But maybe, just maybe, there's a chance that I can take ye by the Ben."

They piled into the car, and Duncan drove off. McKelvie directed him along an unfamiliar route, tortuous and rocky, which climbed the eastern slope of the hills, then turned to the left. When they were halfway up, they reached a point where the car could go no farther. Here, McKelvie leaped out and, without a word, led the way on foot.

They battled through drenched pines and sodden undergrowth, then over crags—half-clambering, half-slipping on the wet, precipitous rock. Duncan's hands were torn and numb.

They were bleeding and breathless when they reached the summit at last. Braced against the sleet-laden wind, his eyes puckered against the darkness, Duncan saw that they had reached the margin of Loch Linton. They had detoured the danger zone and reached to the farther shore of the lake.

"The boat's near here," McKelvie cupped his hands and shouted above the noise of the waves upon the shingle.

A hundred yards along the shore they found the flat-bottom fishing cobble, tossing and pitching at its mooring. They waded out deep and boarded the craft. When McKelvie cast off, each man took an oar.

CHAPTER 58

Almost with relief Duncan put his back into the toil of rowing. The lake was rough, the waves lashed over the skiff's bows. All around was gray darkness.

As the keeper pulled, he swung around from time to time, pointing his nose to the wind, scenting anxiously where they were going. They had been rowing for a long time when all at once McKelvie paused and leaned intently upon his oar. "D'you hear it?" he asked, after a minute.

Above the sounding of the waves, Duncan heard the low rumble of a torrent.

"It's the dam," McKelvie announced with a strange gravity. "God help us if we're caught in that flood."

Turning the boat's nose farther to the wind, they began to pull with greater effort. The roar sounded louder in their ears. But suddenly, as it grew beyond endurance, the boat grounded on the hidden shore and McKelvie, springing out, tugged with his powerful shoulders and beached her.

Beyond the peninsula which bounded the little bay, a smudgy glow hung on the near horizon. With McKelvie at his side, Duncan hurried toward it over the low ridge of the shore. Before them, on the high ground beside the plant, thrown into stark relief by dull red light from a battery of naphtha flares, was a scene which caught Duncan by the throat.

In the background stood the bare structure of the Alumina Works with the new powerhouse and its huddle of sheds and offices. Around the building was a crowd of workmen and village folks—black, motionless figures. In front was the dam, a curving structure of concrete, reinforced with high supporting bastions.

Through the open sluices of the dam a torrent of water boiled and smoked into the darkness of the valley beneath, and over the edge of the coping a solid cascade two hundred feet into the depths below.

But there was a new, more sinister outlet—a wide, jagged break in the smooth facing of the dam, not thirty yards from the nearer bank. Through this the water spouted with truly demoniac force, tearing more chunks of concrete from the edges of the gash.

Duncan was pressing forward, possessed by anxiety to reach Murdoch, when all at once a concerted emotion thrilled the band of onlookers. Duncan swung round in time to view the final cataclysm.

Under his eyes the rent in the rotten wall slowly widened, as though torn apart by a giant's invisible hands. Great slabs of concrete shot through the air like huge projectiles fired from a mammoth gun. The dam slowly wavered in this section, slipped and caved in. And then, like a *papier-mâché* model, the whole structure tottered weakly, swayed, bulged outward, and crumpled finally to nothing beneath the seething cataract of the liberated lake.

"God in Heaven!" gasped McKelvie. "It's like the crack o' doom!"

For an instant Duncan stood stupefied. Then violently he thrust through the mob to the main office of the plant.

There were lights and moving shadows behind the curtained windows. He shivered and with his hand on the door, hesitated. Then the vision came of how Murdoch himself would have entered. He lifted his head and went in.

A number of the Company's officials were in the outer office. Scott was there; the Rev. Simpson; Leggat, the lawyer—all his old enemies from the Levenford Council. And in the center sat Honest Joe, huddled, broken, at his desk. As Duncan entered, he raised his bowed head stupidly. Only one glance passed between the two men. But it was enough for Duncan to read shame and ruin in the defeated eyes. And the abject terror of a gambler who has wagered men's lives and lost.

Duncan advanced toward the room beyond. And there, at last, was the old doctor of Strath Linton.

CHAPTER 59

Murdoch lay on his back upon a couch in the center of the room, covered by a rough brown blanket. By one side of this improvised cot was Jean—pale, drawn, without tears. On the other a youngish man in dark jacket and striped trousers, whom Duncan surmised to be Bailey, the Company doctor.

He tiptoed toward the bed. The old doctor's face, usually so florid, was the color of clay. The immobility of his unconsciousness was terrifying. Wedged beneath his neck was a small sand pillow. As Duncan saw that pillow he looked at the other doctor. In a low voice he said: "I'm Dr. Stirling from Edinburgh. Is it—is it the spine?"

Dr. Bailey, whose worried, indeterminate features showed the strain he had endured that day, made a helpless gesture of assent. "His back, when the stones fell on him." He shuddered. "Broken at the cervical vertebrae. His hip is dislocated, too. He has several fractured ribs. Every bone in his body got it. I think there's internal hemorrhage."

"What have you done?"

"All I could." The tired young doctor was weakly on the defensive. "Hot bottles. Kept him quiet. He can't be moved, or the spinal cord will go." He mumbled: "What more is there to do? He's nearly gone."

With a shock Duncan saw Murdoch's eyes open. A spark of humor flickered into them as he whispered with great effort: "Don't be losin' that infernal temper of yours at Dr. Bailey. He's right. I'm near enough gone."

"Don't talk like that!"

"A dying man maun talk the way he wants," went on Murdoch. "Ye surely see, lad, that this old Adam has seen better days."

A deep sob shook Jean's drooping shoulders. She turned her head away.

"Tut, tut, lass. I didna see you there. It's uncommon dark in this wee room. Give's your hand, my pet, and dinna weep."

Duncan bent forward tensely. "God Almighty, man! You can't give in like this! Jean! Let go your father's hand. Let it go, I say. And leave us alone with him."

The girl rose and stumbled from the room.

Immediately Duncan sank down on one knee in the place she had left. His voice, close to Murdoch's ear, was harshly dissonant. "Murdoch! Have you turned woman in your dotage? Where's your spunk? D'you hear me?"

"Let me be, lad," Murdoch murmured.

"I'll never let you be!" raved Duncan. "For God's sake, pull yourself together." At that he turned down the blanket and with rapid, expert movements ran his hands over the injured man. Bailey was at least a diagnostician.

As his fingers lingered, on a second examination of the broken vertebrae at the base of Murdoch's brain, his mind, working at desperate speed, estimated the chances, gambled on the filament of life that still remained.

CHAPTER 60

Duncan knew, without Dr. Bailey's reminder, the danger even in changing Murdoch's position. One ill-advised shift and the sharp-edged vertebrae would sever the spinal cord, bringing the end instantaneously.

Aid must be given here and now, in this wooden office, without the assistance of skilled nurses, the resource and equipment of a modern operating room. The power of the machine for once was ruthlessly eliminated. All that remained was the power of man.

He rose firmly to his feet, his decision made. All the old, inherent urge came back to him, and with it the buried knowledge of his skill to heal. He saw himself bending over the old doctor, manipulating, drawing the fractured segments into place, easing the tortured spinal nerves, straightening the shattered bones, moving that deadly pressure from the centers in the cord. Swiftly he turned to Bailey.

"You have an anesthetic here? Will you give it?" He stooped down.

"I'm taking an awful chance, Murdoch." He paused, then added with brutal earnestness: "Will you fight back? Or will you let me fail?"

The old doctor gave back the ghostly semblance of a smile. He whispered: "I always swore ye had the knack o' killin' folks. Remember . . . when I don't wake up . . . that I was right."

CHAPTER 61

Five weeks later, a clear January sun broke over the mountains and shone upon the reawakening life of the village of Strath Linton. The solid, stone-built dwellings had stood their ground. High-water marks on whitewashed walls, a few uprooted fences, some broken windows and wrenched-off shutters in process of repair, a torn-up patch in the roadway with a steamroller still parked alongside— these were the only remaining signs of the dreadful flood.

"It'll be fine," thought Provost Dougal, as, poking his beard beyond the lintel of his doorway, he sniffed and cautiously approved the morning.

Down the street came another dignitary, Factor Murray. The two men met soberly, without greeting, and proceeded down the middle of the street.

At first they did not talk—silence in these northern latitudes indicates the elect. But presently the Provost: "I observe in this morning's *Herald* that our friend, Honest Joe, has filed his petition in bankruptcy."

"Ay!" The Factor, a slightly younger man, could not restrain his satisfaction. "He's done for now, the body! Heaven help them that had money in the venture."

"I always maintained that dam of his was foredoomed," remarked the Provost. "Still," he added with native shrewdness, "I'm not sayin' that a proper dam, built respectable-like by a sound concern, wouldn't be an advantage to the district, provided it didn't offshoot to a stenchy aluminum works. We could have beauty and utility alike." He paused impressively. "In fact, I may tell ye, Factor, that such a scheme's in project. Sir John Aigle and his son, the minister, and a few others have got together, and the company'll be formed privately by Martinmas."

"Do ye tell me!" exclaimed the Factor. "Eh, sirs, it's a true word—everything comes to them that waits."

As they passed the Linton Arms, their bearing visibly altered. The Provost looked sadly at the straw-strewn stretch of road that lay before them, and the Factor glanced toward the half-shrouded windows of the doctor's house across the way. Here the two men paused.

The Factor lowered his voice. "The blinds aren't drawn yet. He's had a sore time of it, poor Murdoch."

"Over a month he's lain there," said the Provost gravely. "I'll never forget when they carried him down from the plant—him stricken senseless, strapped on the stretcher."

"They say he hasn't opened an eye in weeks. He just lies there in a stupor. Dear Lord, it's pitiful the way he lingers on."

As they stood watching, they were joined by the schoolmaster, the postman, old Miss Bell in her faded cape, hobbling to open her mercer's store. Soon a small and silent assembly had gathered.

"He has saved so many in his time," grieved the Dominie. "It's hard to see him go like this."

Miss Bell shook her head gloomily. "It seems a cruelty, prolonging the agony this way."

"Ay," agreed the Factor. "It would seem kinder to let him pass, and be done with it."

"We are not the judge o' that, Factor," demurred the Provost. "Doctor Murdoch has been a good friend to this village of Linton. And God will take him when and how He wills."

The Provost shook his head slowly, a sign which dispersed the gathering. They parted with a nod, and each went upon his way.

CHAPTER 62

Inside that silent, oppressive house, a door opened. Duncan emerged from the sick man's room. He was unshaven, and lines of fatigue were deep beneath his eyes. He had spent most of the night by Murdoch's bedside, where, a moment ago, Jean had relieved him. The vigil, one of many, had taxed him to the point of collapse.

He placed his arm against the wall and sank his head upon it. How proud he had been, after his long manipulation at the hut, to set the broken bones and still maintain the spark of life! How utterly cast down to see this fatal and persistent coma follow, from which it seemed nothing but death could rouse the injured man.

Five heartbreaking, interminable weeks he had spent at Linton, without once returning to Edinburgh. His mind, remotely aware of that other existence, of his work at the Foundation, of all his obligations and opportunities there, was nevertheless fettered by the task of tending Murdoch. Yet all that he had done, all that could be done, seemed wasted effort.

In the quiet of the house there came the muted ring of the telephone. He heard the tiptoed step of Retta as she went to answer it. He sighed, roused himself with an effort, went downstairs.

"Yes, Retta?" he asked. "A call?"

"No, doctor. It was Edinburgh again. There's no stopping them. But I did as you said—told them you weren't available."

He nodded. "Quite right. If they call again, tell them the same thing."

That morning the round was not heavy. In the present circumstances, since Dr. Bailey had resigned and the whole practice was again Murdoch's, only the gravest and most urgent cases applied for medical attention.

On his last visit, after he had ministered to his patient, Duncan was followed to the door by the woman of the house. She looked at him with deep concern in her honest country face, then asked the universal question. "How is Dr. Murdoch today?"

He answered mechanically. "As well as can be expected."

"Tell me, doctor, do you think that he'll get better?"

Something made him drop his noncommittal formula. "I don't think so," he said. "Though God knows I'm doing my best."

"We all know that, doctor." She nodded slowly. "And, believe me, that's good enough for us."

As he drove to the village, that word of homely praise remained with him, warm and comforting, a small and secret afterglow in the fog of his despair.

CHAPTER 63

It was after one when he got back. Drawn up outside Murdoch's house was a large, closed, hired car. His mouth came together in a grim line. He knew what it meant, even before he went into the house and found Anna, seated in the little back surgery, impatiently smoking a cigarette.

"Well, Anna." He greeted her calmly. "I thought I told you not to come. After all those wires and phone calls, I felt you'd have understood."

"Wires you don't answer! And phone calls you ignore!" She crushed her cigarette viciously in the ashtray. "Can you blame me for wishing the delightful pleasure of a heart-to-heart talk?"

He shrugged his shoulders, then went to the little dispensary in the corner. Standing there, at the tiny bench with its cracked sink, he began to make up, from the few drugs upon the shelves, the simple medicines he had prescribed for his patients that morning. The sight seemed to destroy the remnants of her control.

"Duncan!" she exclaimed. "Are you completely insane—dishing out colored water in this wretched wooden shack, when you might be working in your own laboratory?"

"There's an ingredient in this colored water that you wouldn't understand."

"What ingredient?" she snapped.

"Faith," he answered quietly.

She stared at him with furious, disdainful eyes. "You have gone crazy! Jeopardizing your entire career to sell mythical virtues to gaping country patients."

"Maybe," he interrupted her harshly. "But I have another patient—who happens to be upstairs."

"I know. I have seen him. Yes, you needn't glare like that! I took the liberty of making an examination in your absence. And I tell you, you are wasting your time."

146

He flinched as if she had passed sentence of death upon him. "You'd naturally take that view."

"I take the unbiased, scientific view. There is edema of the brain. That poor old man upstairs is fit only for the churchyard. And all the faith you can pump into him won't change it."

"What right have you to talk like that?"

"The right of a scientist—who is your friend. Oh, I know what you've done—set the spine, kept him alive with artificial feeding, watched him day and night. It's commendable. But it's useless, utterly useless. The best thing you could do for him would be to walk out of this house and order his tombstone."

The hand that held the measuring glass shook slightly. "You're a hard woman, Anna."

"In my job, and yours, can we be otherwise?" Her voice quivered. "Listen to me! And try to see things sanely—just this once. It was bad enough, losing your golden opportunity to dine with the Commission. But your absence from the Department during the last five weeks, before the election, letting them all get ahead of you—it's been suicidal. I needn't tell you how Overton has taken advantage of it. I've tried my best, explained to Professor Lee, exploited the emotional aspect of the case to the Commission till I'm tired. Now—" she paused—"explanations are no longer any use. The applicants come up for interview tomorrow. Has that penetrated? The letter's at your rooms. The election takes place tomorrow afternoon at three o'clock." She emphasized each word, as one might instruct a child. "You must—you must be there. At the Foundation, three o'clock, tomorrow."

CHAPTER 64

He corked a bottle of physic, labeled it, and placed it upon the ledge. He said slowly: "Of course I'll try to get in. But I can't promise to be there, because if I do, they'll keep me there—I'll be swallowed up. And you know I've made up my mind to see this out, here, the way Murdoch would stick to a case like this himself—to the very end."

She bit her lip fiercely. "The end! Haven't I told you? It's futile. From you, a trained pathologist—"

He swung round. "There are certain things in doctoring you don't find in a test tube. And one of them is: Don't desert your patient—until he's dead."

"You sentimental fool!" She was angrier than he had ever seen her. "If you're arguing on that plane, don't you owe me anything? You, with your faith, hope, and charity, your notions of gratitude! Why don't you pay me back for what I've done for you?"

He said slowly, "I'd rather give you back my arm—than Murdoch's life."

All at once her anger vanished. "Is that all you have to say to me, Duncan? After all our years together?"

He stared at her, uncomprehending.

"I mean," she faltered, "why should we ever quarrel? It hurts!"

"That's a strange remark from you."

"Perhaps I'm a strange woman. You don't know how strange—I don't even know, myself. You think I'm hard. God knows—these last months, I've turned weaker even than your silly Margaret."

She lowered her eyes, then suddenly raised them again, filled with an irrepressible yearning. "Sometimes we sneer at the things we long for most. But there comes a time when we can't deny them, when we can't go on stamping out the fire. We've been together a long time now, Duncan. We've both been knocked about by life. We have a common objective—we're linked together. Duncan, I'm desperately bound up in everything that happens to you. I'm—" her voice wavered—"rather fond of you. Couldn't we work out something for our future? Oh, what a mess I'm making of this! But you mean a lot to me. And surely I must mean something to you, too."

He looked away, and said with difficulty, "I value your friendship more than anything that's left to me."

She stood very still for a moment. Then she rose, fumbling with the fastenings of her cloak. Her face was quiet, expressionless again.

"Well, we needn't continue this conversation, and I promise you I won't renew it. But you're coming tomorrow. That's settled. There's just one thing more—Nurse Dawson's letters."

He shook his head. "No, Anna. I won't use them."

She seemed upon the point of a final outburst. "Tomorrow will be time enough. I'll meet you at the Foundation. Three o'clock. You won't forget it?"

"No. But I may not be there."

"You'll be there," she answered. "You're too ambitious, and so am I, to miss the chance of a lifetime. Good-bye—till tomorrow."

She nodded with her old firmness, that same hypnotic sparkle in her eye, and then she was gone.

CHAPTER 65

Next morning Duncan awakened to a racking sense of tension. His room was next to Murdoch's, and from habit, almost before his eyes were open, he listened for sounds in the adjoining room. He heard the district nurse relieve Jean from her spell of duty. Driven by his vague unease, he jumped out of bed, shaved, and dressed quickly. Early in the forenoon he had a very serious case at the Rossdhu Forestry Station, thirty miles up the glen. But first he went to see his patient.

Nurse Gordon, a thickset, middle-aged woman in a faded blue uniform, her plain, efficient features stamped with the record of her ten years' service in the district, had almost finished her ministrations as he entered. She whispered: "He's not so well this morning, doctor. I'm thinking, if anything, he's weaker."

Duncan placed his fingers on Murdoch's wrist, made his routine examination. What she had said was true. He scanned the chart she had placed on the table and wrote his instructions.

Downstairs he snatched a mouthful of breakfast and then hurried to the garage, started the car, and left upon his visit.

Deep down, he knew why he craved urgent and distracting action. It was a desperate desire to escape—from himself, from Murdoch, from the crisis that involved them both.

When he returned, Jean met him in the hall, neat in her gray gown and fresh despite her pallor and the dark shadows of sadness beneath her eyes.

Beyond the surprise of seeing her—she had been up all night and should have been in bed—her presence caused him a stab of pain. He knew now beyond all shadow of doubt that he loved her. It was the real thing, unswerving and irrevocable, at last. But he could not forget her attachment to young Aigle.

"Why aren't you resting?" He had to steady himself to meet her gaze.

"I'm not the least tired." She forced a reassuring smile. "Perhaps I'll lie down when Nurse Gordon comes back at one o'clock. I thought we'd have lunch early."

He had no appetite. When he had done his best with the chicken, she offered him a dish of hothouse grapes.

"Do try these," she urged. "Sir John Aigle sent them from his own greenhouses."

He shook his head. More than ever, the name of Aigle sent a wave of resentment over him. Sir John was always sending flowers and fruit, both quite useless, Duncan thought scornfully, to the unconscious Murdoch.

"They're very good." She seemed disappointed because he would not taste the grapes. "We owe Sir John a lot."

"I daresay." A bitter impulse seized him, and he added, "But I've no wish to be indebted to him."

"I'm sorry. He means well." She hesitated, then made herself go on. "He told me he would arrange for father's medical attention, if you had to go."

He stared at her, stunned that she should have seen the secret torment of his mind.

"You see, obviously you can't stay here forever. We're very grateful to you for all you've done." Her smile was a shadow of its normal brightness. "But now, there seems so little more that you can do."

He saw it all, as clear as noonday sun—the reason for her nervousness, her attempt at lightness. Anna had spoken to her yesterday, and Jean was opening the gates for him, the gates of freedom.

Even as the thought flashed across his mind, Hamish knocked and, cap in hand, entered the room.

"I have your suitcase here, Dr. Stirling. Shall I put it in the car now?"

"Leave it in the hall a moment, Hamish." He was shaken with the realization that in the next few seconds he must make the decision that would determine his entire future.

CHAPTER 66

When Hamish had gone, he fixed his gaze upon Jean. Although he recognized her unselfishness, he had a perverse desire to hurt her.

"Kind of you to plan the farewell banquet, with the help of the Aigles."

Her voice was unsteady as she answered. "I wanted to give you time to get to Edinburgh by three."

He could not stop. "Very thoughtful, considering that I haven't exactly distinguished myself with your father's case. I've failed. And you know I've failed."

She whispered, "I've already told you—"

He interrupted shortly: "That you want to get rid of me. Well, I daresay you're right. I don't blame you."

He could not understand what drove him to hurt her. He had never loved her more than at this moment. After her weeks of nursing, her nights and days of hopes and fears, she had a strangely childlike quality. He continued in spite of himself. "I won't stay where I'm not wanted." He got up from the table. "Give me five minutes, and I'll be gone."

Out in the hall he found his suitcase with his coat and hat laid across it. Through the glass panel of the front door he saw the car outside, with Hamish waiting at the wheel. He could be in Edinburgh with ease by half past two.

He saw himself returning to the great city. He saw his dramatic arrival at the Foundation, his welcome by his friends, the discomfiture of Overton. He couldn't let Overton win. Anna was right. He decided there and then that he would leave. But something made him go upstairs to take a final look at Murdoch.

The sickroom was still and dim. Murdoch still lay on his back, unconscious, helpless, as he had lain for these past five weeks of living death.

If only he had driven off the torpor, brought back his

152

patient from the trance, all would have been well. He had not done so. The room was so quiet he could hear the ticking of his watch, drawing him swiftly toward the hour of his appointment. He had been told to go. The dying man would never miss him.

Still he remained. He could not take his eyes from the shadowed outline of Murdoch's face. There must be something he could do for him.

Only the stimulus of his present mood could have flashed to Duncan an expedient as desperate as the one he thought of then. He knew the danger. He trembled even as he thought of it. But it was an aspiration of the brain or nothing. Death would come if nothing were attempted.

He worked out the details of the treatment, tensely awaiting the arrival of the district nurse. She came in noiselessly, at precisely one o'clock.

As she took off her cloak, she studied Murdoch's face, then said quietly to Duncan: "Miss Jean said to remind you it's time that you were going. Or else you may be late."

He answered tautly. "Yes, I daresay I may be late. Nurse Gordon, will you get the spirit kettle going? Then sterilize my instruments, please."

She glanced at him and again at Murdoch. Then she went to do his bidding. "All ready then, Dr. Stirling," she said at length.

Together they turned Murdoch over gently. He lay on his side, his back toward them, the worn-out hulk of what once had been a man. First with alcohol, than with picric, Duncan thoroughly swabbed the basal region. The smear showed greenish yellow against the sickly white of Murdoch's skin.

CHAPTER 67

Slowly Duncan's fingers moved about the base of the brain. He felt the union of the injured vertebrae; it was firm and complete. Laterally, he chose the vital spot. Without removing his index finger, he slewed round and picked up the trocar—a tubed needle with an interior stilette, a shining dagger with which he must pierce into the vital tissues of the medulla. One mistake would be sufficient, the slightest error in distance or direction—he knew exactly how terribly the end would come. Nurse Gordon knew it, too.

Tensing the patient's skin between his thumb and forefinger, Duncan plunged the trocar into the unresistant flesh. For a long, full minute he worked the unseen point of the instrument backward, forward, searching for the point of insertion. And always he met with resistance. Could he never find the opening?

Desperately he closed his eyes to increase his sensitiveness of touch. He tried again. And again. Then he cried out with relief. This time there was no obstruction—the needle glided swiftly forward. He had found the orifice. Gently he guided the needle into the canal.

Carefully, guardedly, he went deeper. His face was masklike. It was no surgeon's work that he was doing, no exhibition of textbook technique. He was using the gift God had given him. Onward he went. Suddenly he felt the snick as the trocar pierced the thecal membrane. He had reached his objective.

It was the moment, the crisis that would prove whether he was right or wrong, whether Murdoch must live or die. With a quick pull he withdrew the stilette from the hollow needle.

Instantly, at hypertension force, a gush of cerebrospinal fluid spouted through the needle.

But, though Duncan saw his action to be justified, he did

not dare to hope. The fluid came more strongly; the pressure within was manifestly intense. And suddenly from Murdoch there came a long, faint sigh, the first sound he had uttered since he lapsed into coma five long weeks before.

Nurse Gordon almost dropped the receiver. "Dr. Stirling," she gasped. "Did you hear?"

Duncan did not answer. His lips were dry and stiff with suspense. He watched the needle fixedly. The fluid dripped slowly, then more slowly, and finally it ceased to flow.

Quickly he withdrew the needle, sealed the puncture with collodion, and again turned Murdoch upon his back. He waited while the nurse slipped two pillows behind the patient's head; then he held a vial of sal ammoniac beneath the sick man's nose. The stimulant had no effect.

Duncan fought back despair. Leaning over, he pressed firmly with both thumbs on Murdoch's brow, over the track of the supraorbital nerves—a device he had often used to bring his patients round from deep anesthesia. For a minute—nothing. Then, as he increased the pressure, the unbelievable took place. Murdoch slowly opened his eyes.

CHAPTER 68

It was like the dead returning to life. With one hand to her mouth, Nurse Gordon let out a stifled scream. Hushed though it was, the old man seemed to hear it.

"What's wrong?" he whispered feebly.

Duncan bent forward, a great exhilaration singing in his ears. "Nothing," he said reassuringly. "Don't excite yourself for anything."

Murdoch weakly focused his eyes on Duncan. "You're still here," he muttered, and at the old, familiar irony, Duncan wanted to shout aloud.

"Please, Dr. Murdoch," Nurse Gordon begged. "You mustn't talk too much; you must rest."

"I think I've rested long enough," mumbled the old man. "Pull up the blinds and let me see the light."

Duncan dashed to the window and pulled the cord. The nurse, beside herself, was not to be outdone. She offered Murdoch a cup of milk.

"Whatna mush is that? I think I could relish some strong beef tea."

"Yes, yes—to be sure. I'll see about it." Duncan seized the excuse to leave the room. He could not bear this crashing ecstasy. Murdoch, his dear old friend, arisen unbelievably from the grave.

Out on the landing he made an effort to compose himself before he hurried downstairs.

"Jean!" he called. "Your father's better! Jean! Jean!"

He thought she might be in the garden and rushed out through the front door, hatless and in his shirt sleeves.

She was not there; but up the street a little way there stood the usual afternoon gathering of villagers. The Provost was there, and Factor Murray, the Dominie, Farmer Blair, Hamish, and a dozen others of importance in the community. They were silent as they watched Duncan come toward them.

"Murdoch!" said the Provost in a stricken voice. "He's passed away at last."

"No, Provost, no," Duncan shouted. "He's taken the turn. He'll win through!"

They gazed at him in silence.

"Do ye—can ye mean it, doctor?" asked the Provost at last.

"Mean it!" Duncan's voice cracked. "He's through the coma. He talked with me—a minute ago. He's asked for beef tea."

A shout went up. Stepping forward, Provost Dougal gripped Duncan's hand in his, all his feelings contained in that hard clasp. Then he swung round. "Robert, run with the news. Get Hamish to ring the bells. Run, lad, run! As for us—" his moist eyes swept the group—"let every man give praise."

Their hymn was sounding in Duncan's ears as he raced back into the house. As he entered, the bells began to ring wildly, bearing the tidings to all the Strath.

"Jean!" He called, crossing the hall. "Jean! Jean!"

She came from her father's room, closed the door, her thin, pale face transfigured. He hastened forward; but before he could reach her, she had fainted.

CHAPTER 69

The passing of a bare twelve days had brought a great change upon the doctor's house. Windows and doors were wide open to the early-spring sunshine. The chickens strutted in the back yard; the garden was showing tender green, and the sound of Retta's voice as she sang a Gaelic air came blithely from the scullery. In the kitchen, busily engaged in jam making—there was nothing Murdoch relished more than marmalade preserve—was Jean.

As she sliced the oranges and popped them with sugar into the copper pan, her face, though grave, was happy.

Suddenly a sharp knocking made her stop. At first she thought it was her father, who, armed with a stick, was now heartily convalescent in his bedroom and did not scruple to rap loudly on the floor above when he needed her.

It was not Murdoch, however, but someone at the front door. She went, without troubling to unpin her apron, and there was young Aigle.

"Alex!" she exclaimed. "You're home!"

"Jean!" He took both her hands in his, as if he would never let them go. "I got in this morning. Only just heard about all you've been through. I couldn't come over quickly enough."

"That was like you, Alex." She smiled. "How well you're looking—tanned and quite American."

He studied her with concern. "You're bonnier than ever, Jean; but you're paler, thinner."

"I'm fine." She laughed away his solicitude. "You should have seen me a fortnight ago. But look here, young man!" She disengaged her hands. "My marmalade'll burn if I don't look out. Away up and see Father. You'll find me in the kitchen when you come down."

While he ran up the stairs, two at a time, she returned to her jam-making. From time to time she heard their voices.

Then in half an hour Alex returned. "My word!" he declared. "He's wonderful! I never thought to find him half so fit." He seated himself on the table, watching her as she stirred the marmalade.

"It seems to me, Jean, you owe a lot to Dr. Stirling."

"We do," she answered quietly.

"From what I can gather," he went on with some difficulty, "Stirling stopped on here, practically saved your father's life, when he might have been in Edinburgh getting the Foundation Chair. By the way, who did get that appointment, Jean?"

"I don't know. It hasn't been announced yet. But remember, Dr. Stirling made the sacrifice in spite of me and everybody else."

"He's a fine fellow." Alex paused, frowning. "But—well, rather a queer one."

She said quickly, "Aren't we all a little queer, Alex?"

"When does he leave?"

"Soon, I expect." Her eyes were downcast. "You see, he understands that Dad'll never be fit for hard work again. He's waiting until we make arrangements for the future."

Aigle moved from the table, advanced toward her. "Jean! My dear! Let me help you with those arrangements. That's why I've rushed over to you." His voice took on a deeper earnestness. "Let me take care of your father, and you. Marry me, Jean. You know—I've told it to you so often—I love you very much."

She was so still he thought his argument had moved her. Then she shook her head, stifling his protestations by her quietness. He seemed so young to her—not without character, but stereotyped and immature. "I'm sorry, Alex. I like you such a lot. And you and Sir John have always been so kind, so wonderful to us. If only I loved you." Her eyes were troubled when she turned to him. "But I don't, Alex. And it's best that you should know it. I'm sorry, Alex dear."

There were lines of despondency in his face. But as she looked at him in affectionate distress, she could not help feeling that he would soon get over it.

"Cheer up, Alex." She gave his hand a quick, maternal pat. "It won't seem so bad in six weeks' time."

"Six years is more like it."

Alex remained a few minutes. Then, as though relieved that this concession to convention was accomplished, he gave her a quick, embarrassed glance, shook her hand, and hurriedly left.

CHAPTER 70

A moment later the door reopened. She glanced up, thinking he had returned. But it was Duncan, back from his round. He seemed older, somehow, erect and rugged, with a quiet, new assurance.

Watching her intently, he said: "I saw young Aigle departing. From the speed of his car, you'd have thought he'd just been given the earth."

She colored to the roots of her hair at his misconception. The knowledge of her flush made her angry with herself, so increased her confusion that she could not say a word. He glanced at her again, confirmed in his false surmise. "So that's the way of it," he thought.

"There's something I'd like to discuss with you," he said. "It's about the practice. I don't want to worry your father; but if he wished, I'd be glad to take it over. I'd do all the work, of course. He could remain in a purely advisory capacity. As for the money—that doesn't matter. Anything would be agreeable to me."

She was too astonished to answer. As she saw his set expression, she thought, "Here is a man whom I love beyond endurance and whom, also, I could fear." She faltered, stung by a sense of blame. "If it hadn't been for us," she said, "you'd still be in Edinburgh, making a great name for yourself. It was our fault, my fault, that you lost the Wallace Chair. And now, out of charity and pity, you're offering to do this!"

"You're quite wrong. Yesterday they offered me the Chair, and I refused it."

He took a letter from his pocket and handed it to her. It was a formal letter, offering him the Principalship of the Foundation.

She gasped. "They knew, then, why you stayed here. This—this is wonderful!"

He took the letter and dropped it into the fire. "Maybe," he said quietly. "But not for me."

"Duncan! What do you mean?"

"You say these last weeks have ruined my life. That isn't true. On the contrary, they've remade my life—shown me the way I must go." He took a long breath. "Ever since I qualified, except for one short month down here, I've been lost, groping in a long, dark tunnel, driven by a false ambition. I was caught—caught by the machine—untrue to myself, being punched out to pattern like the others. Your father was dead right, Jean. What do I want with monographs, test tubes, burettes, spectroscopes, electrocardiographs, galvanometers, and all the rest? Oh, they have their uses, no doubt, though it's all exaggerated. But my place isn't beside them. I'm not made that way.

"I want to heal people, and I know I'm made to heal them. I want to go into their homes, and ease their suffering, bring them back from the gates of death—with the power that God has given me." He paused, then continued more calmly. "As for Strath Linton—I love it. These decent folks here—they're my own kind. And I love the outdoor life. They can keep their cities. All that I want is here."

CHAPTER 71

"And so," she said unsteadily, you're going to stay."

"Yes. And incidentally, by doing so, I'll pay another debt. If I stand aside, they'll give the Principalship—not to Overton—but to Anna. Yes, despite the fact that she's a woman. They respect her capabilities. That'll be a grand thing for the Foundation. And for her." He hesitated. "So I'll be here to dance at your wedding. Clown that I am, I should have congratulated you. He's a good fellow, Alex." He tried to joke. "When you're Lady Aigle, don't dare look down your nose at the doctor of the glen." He turned to go.

"I'll never marry Alex Aigle—never, never!" Jean said. She wanted to burst into tears.

He stopped abruptly. "Why?"

Nothing mattered but that he should know. She turned away blindly. "Because I love someone else."

For an instant he did not move. Then slowly, uncertainly, he came forward, a great hope in his eyes. "Jean! You wouldn't—by any chance—mean me?"

She swung round, tears running down her cheeks. "I've loved you from that first minute I saw you in the rain."

"Jean!" he cried. "My own dear Jean!"

They were in each other's arms. He murmured: "I never thought I had a chance, Jean. For months I've had you in my heart—ever since I found myself."

She lifted her face. He kissed her, and she lay in his arms while time dissolved and the ages fled. Then she smiled, as a rapping came from the room upstairs. Louder it came, and more impatient.

"Father," Jean whispered. "Let's go tell him, now, together."

On a fine June afternoon, more than a year later, an unusual stir centered round the house of the doctor of Strath Linton. There were fresh curtains on the spotless windows, a brand-new mat inside the porch, scarlet geraniums in the front flowerbed, and the smell of new-baked cakes, pies, fat roasting fowls, and gooseberry tarts. Every now and then footsteps scurried within.

Outside, however, in the front garden, seated in camp chairs on either side of the raked path, in a position to command full view of the village street, were two persons apparently at ease. Murdoch, in fine broadcloth, white-haired, but still hale and hearty, was one of them. The other, more upright, severe and prim in her best black gown, bonnet on head, umbrella in hand, her formidable features relaxed, yet barely admitting her present satisfaction, was Martha, Duncan's mother.

CHAPTER 72

There she sat, glancing round the pleasant scene—mountains, moor, river, and the nearby village—as though she had never uttered one harsh word in all her life. Presently she remarked, trying to hide her nervousness, "Though I say it myself, it's a braw day for a christening."

The old doctor had already found the joy of contradicting her. "It'll rain before night."

"It will not," she disagreed. "Not on the christening o' my grandson."

"Your grandson, indeed." He pretended to laugh. "Have I no rights in the matter? The bairn's the image of me."

"God forbid!" she exclaimed piously. "I wouldna wish such a misfortune on any babe—let alone my own son's firstborn. No, no, this is a braw bairn. He has my color of eyes and the Stirling nose.

Murdoch chuckled. "Ye needn't glower at me, woman. I'm not feared of you like your poor Duncan, whom you cut off from ye for all those years."

Her face softened. "That's a long story," she said. "He disobeyed me, ye ken."

"Well, wasn't he justified?"

She shook her head stubbornly. "He might ha' done better if he'd taken my advice. But I'm prepared to forgive him now. I made up my mind this morning for the sake of the bairn. Can I say more?"

"Can ye say more?" He gasped with laughter. "God save us, woman, but ye're generous! If I were Duncan, I'd send ye packing. Ay, and maybe when he knows you're here, he will."

His reassuring guffaw stopped only when Long Tom, dressed in a tailcoat much too large for his spare figure, came sauntering up the path.

Martha glared at her husband. "Mind you, you're not to

drink at the christening," she said severely. "Not one drop!"

Long Tom fingered with pride the gold chain that anchored his fine new watch in his waistcoat pocket—a present from Duncan, who would never forget that his father had given him his watch when he first set out for Edinburgh. "Nothing stronger nor water," he said.

"Only champagne," Murdoch suggested. "We'll split a bottle between us, Tom. It's no more than ginger ale."

A step behind them stopped further argument. Jean stood on the porch, smiling, with the baby, in his long white christening robe, in her arms.

"Indeed," the old woman said with a proud smile, "he's a lovely boy."

"That's one thing we all agree on," Long Tom observed gently.

"Goodness!" Jean glanced toward the street. "Here's the visitors coming, and Duncan never home."

The first pair of guests came sedately up the path: Provost Dougal and the Dominie in their Sabbath clothes. Close behind them were the Factor, Miss Bell, the McKelvies, Reid, and the minister. Soon the porch was crowded.

The Provost coughed, breaking an awkward silence. "That's a nasty cough ye have, Provost," remarked Murdoch with a professional air. "I'll give ye something for it."

"Ye needna trouble, mon," answered the Provost unthinkingly. "After the ceremony, I'm goin' to get it from the doctor himself."

"What!" Murdoch roared, and everyone laughed delightedly. "Where is the doctor that ye talk about? Can he not come home for his own son's christening?"

Jean apologized. "He had an extra long round today—to the head of the Strath."

Just then they heard the sound of a car. In a moment the doctor of the glen, followed by Hamish, ran up the driveway, his eyes kindling at the sight of his guests, his wife, his new son. Even in one year his work had set its mark upon him. There was deep humanity in the stern, kindly face, now

166

weathered to a healthy bronze, and his figure in its rough tweed suit was burlier than before.

He reached the group, smiled upon them with the serenity of a man who has found himself. He did not see his mother, who had shrunk behind the others in sudden nervousness.

CHAPTER 73

"I'm sorry to be late. I had an unexpected appendectomy at Rossdhu." He glanced at his wife. "And I was stopped on my way home." He handed Jean an open telegram.

She read it aloud: "Am with you in spirit today. You were right, damn you. Kiss the baby for his dusty old aunt. Love to Jean and a handclasp to yourself from the weary Principal of the Wallace Foundation. Anna Geisler."

A look of perfect understanding passed between Duncan and Jean. Then she said softly, "There's someone here you haven't seen." Turning, she took Martha's hand and drew her forward.

"Mother!"

For a moment they faced each other; then she looked away, ashamed.

"I thought I'd come. I've keepit my things on. If I'm not wanted, I'll go home."

Murdoch blew his nose in tactful intervention and, taking Long Tom's arm, guided the guests inside.

Duncan was left alone with his mother and Jean.

"I must say—" the old woman struggled on—"I'm glad to see ye so happy and successful, with your wife and all."

He stepped forward and put his arm around her. "Mother, we're all glad to see you!"

Martha, fighting back her tears, tried to speak and could not. For the first time in many years, she wept. "Maybe, my dear lad, maybe we both were right," she conceded, drying her eyes. "Can I go in and hold the bairn?"

Duncan nodded happily. And with one arm about his mother's shoulders, the other round his wife's waist, he led them into the house.

Made in the USA
Las Vegas, NV
16 February 2024

85891334R00100